The Escape

Even the book morphs!
Flip the pages
and check it out!

Look for other **ANIMORPHS**®
titles by K.A. Applegate:

#1 The Invasion
#2 The Visitor
#3 The Encounter
#4 The Message
#5 The Predator
#6 The Capture
#7 The Stranger
#8 The Alien
#9 The Secret
#10 The Android
#11 The Forgotten
#12 The Reaction
#13 The Change
#14 The Unknown
#15 The Escape
#16 The Warning
#17 The Underground

<MEGAMORPHS>
#1 The Andalite's Gift

the andalite chronicles

ANIMORPHS®

The Escape

K.A. Applegate

AN
APPLE
PAPERBACK

SCHOLASTIC INC.
New York Toronto London Auckland Sydney

For big Michael and little Jake

No part of this publication may be reproduced in whole or in part, or stored in a retrieval system, or transmitted in any form or by any means, electronic, mechanical, photocopying, recording, or otherwise, without written permission of the publisher. For information regarding permission, write to Scholastic Inc., Attention: Permissions Department, 555 Broadway, New York, NY 10012.

ISBN 0-590-49424-4

12 11 10 9 8 7   8 9/9 0 1 2 3/0

Printed in the U.S.A.   40

First Scholastic printing, January 1998

CHAPTER 1

My name is Marco.

I've always kind of liked my name. Marco. It brings Marco Polo to mind. Not that my last name is Polo. Or maybe it is. I'm not going to tell you.

None of us will tell you our last names. None of us Animorphs. Or where we live. Or anything else that would help the Yeerks find us.

Yeerks? *What are Yeerks?* you wonder.

I'll tell you. They are a species of parasites. Like tapeworms, only worse. See, Yeerks don't just crawl up inside your stomach or intestines. They crawl inside your brain. They sink their malleable bodies into the nooks and crannies of your brain. They tie straight into your brain's neurons.

1

They control your brain. They control you more completely than it is possible for you to imagine.

You think, *Oh, well, I would still be able to keep control over myself.* But you'd be wrong. See, if you had a Yeerk in your head right now, it would be the Yeerk that would be moving your hands and fingers; the Yeerk who'd be focusing your eyes; the Yeerk who'd be deciding if you were hungry.

The Yeerks enter your brain and make you a slave. They open your memories and read them like a book. You can still think, sure. You can still feel. You can be afraid or angry or humiliated. But you can do nothing on your own. It is a slavery more total than any ever experienced on Earth. But then, the Yeerks aren't from Earth.

People with Yeerks in their heads are called Controllers. Human-Controllers, if the Yeerk has taken over a human. Hork-Bajir-Controllers, when the victim is a Hork-Bajir. Although pretty much all Hork-Bajir are Controllers, so we don't really bother to say "Hork-Bajir-Controllers."

We fight the Yeerk invasion led by the evil creature, Visser Three. Five human kids and an Andalite kid. We're the only people who know what's happening. Just us. And the Yeerks, of course.

And how do we fight? With the morphing power given to us by a dying Andalite prince. The power to become any animal we can touch.

The power to morph.

How do you know who is a Controller and who isn't? That's the problem. You don't. You can look deep into the eyes of the person you trust most and never, ever guess that behind those eyes is an alien parasite.

Now you know why I won't tell you my last name. Or where I live. Not even what state. See, I want to live. I want to live to fight.

And one day, I want to live to rescue the one person who matters most to me. The person whose eyes I looked into for years without knowing she was no longer my mother.

But being an Animorph is not always danger and battle. There are other times when the powers we possess can be useful. Even fun.

And on a nice Wednesday afternoon after school, I was at the mall with the others, doing just that: having fun. And we weren't at the usual, everyday mall. This was the new, massive Mega Mall they'd built across town.

It was Cassie's idea, oddly enough. Normally she'd be the last person to ever cook up a hare-brained scheme. But this involved mistreating animals. And you don't want to mess with animals when Cassie is around.

"Squuuaaaakk! The food is good! The food is good! Squuuaaakkk!"

It was me, Jake, Cassie, Tobias, Rachel, and

3

Ax. Ax was in human morph, of course. So was Tobias. Tobias has regained his ability to morph now, but he's still a red-tailed hawk. He can morph into his old human shape, but if he stays in that shape more than two hours, he'll be trapped in it and never be able to morph again. He made the choice to live as a hawk and keep his morphing power.

I don't know if I'd have been tough enough to make that choice.

As for Ax, well, he's an Andalite. He has a human morph he uses sometimes. He was using it now, fortunately, or otherwise there would have been a lot of screaming and panicking and general weirding-out. An Andalite walking around the mall is something you notice.

"Squuuaaaakkkk! Try the Rain Forest burger. It's squuuaaaakkk good!"

In this mall was a restaurant called the Amazon Cafe. It was a cool restaurant because it was like going on some ride at Disney World. The tables were totally surrounded by plants and stuff arranged to look like a jungle. There were lots of fake birds and fake alligators and fake snakes in fake trees.

Unfortunately, there were also some real birds. Parrots, to be exact. These parrots were out where people wait in line to get a table. They were on perches, surrounded by people. Old people, young people, cool people, annoying people. People who would try to scare the birds or feed them garbage or poke them with cigarette butts.

Which annoyed Cassie. It annoyed her so badly she had come to me and asked, "Marco, what can I do to save those poor birds? They aren't allowed any dignity!"

And I had said, "Hmmm. Parrots, right? They talk, right?"

"Yeah. Why? Do you have an idea?"

"Oh, yes. I have a definite idea."

And now, a couple days after that conversation, we were at the mall. And we were right in the forefront of people annoying the parrots.

"Say 'Howard Stern rules!'" a kid urged a bright green parrot.

"Squuuaaaakkk! Amazon Cafe! It's an adventure!"

"No, idiot bird dude, Howard Stern rules, man! Say 'Howard Stern rules!'"

"Moron," Rachel sneered.

The kid turned to her. "Yeah, this bird is a total moron."

"I wasn't talking about the bird, you —"

Jake put his hand on Rachel's shoulder, quieting her down. Rachel has an occasional problem with anger. And she has no tolerance for jerks.

Rachel is tall and blond and beautiful and totally without fear. Now, sure, way down inside she's also insecure, scared by her own inability to fit in, and way too pressured to live up to her own high standards. But all that stuff is way down inside. Way down so far that if you ever tried to reach it, she'd have sliced and diced you before you even got close.

"Okay, let's do this," Jake said. "It's almost time for them to clean the parrot perches, if Cassie's timing is right."

"Every day at this time," Cassie assured us. "In fact, here comes the woman who does it."

I saw a twenty-something woman in a waitress uniform coming toward us. She was carrying a large wire cage.

"Squuuuaaaakkk! Pot stickers! Pot stickers! Squuuaaaakkkk!"

"Okay, we're straight on this? Rachel, Marco, Cassie, and me, follow her to the back. Tobias and Ax, you stay here as backup."

"Backup," Ax agreed. "Ba-kup. Bakkup. Look! Is that the place where cinnamon buns are created? Oh, cinnamon buns. Bunzuh."

Jake sighed. "Maybe after we're done we could go to Cinnabon," he said in his talking-to-lunatics voice.

See, in his own body, Ax has no mouth. Andalites talk by thought-speech and eat through their hooves. So when he's human, the Ax-man can get a little weird about spoken sounds. And a lot weird about flavor. And utterly insane when exposed to cinnamon buns, which, as far as Ax is concerned, are the finest things the human race has ever created. Forget music and art. Ax would trade a Cinnabon for the Mona Lisa, straight across.

"Okay, she's going!" Cassie warned.

The woman had stuffed the four parrots into the cage and was heading back into the restaurant. We followed her.

"Duh duh, duh duh, duh duh, duh duh, duh duh," I sang, doing the theme from *Mission: Impossible.* "Your mission, should you decide to accept it: Give the parrots back their dignity and strike a blow for Mommy Earth!"

Cassie rolled her eyes at me. Jake hid a smile.

"I can't believe you're going along with this, Jake. Responsible Jake giving his okay to a totally personal use of our powers. Never thought I'd see the day," I teased him. "It's 'cause he really likes Cassie," I added to Rachel in a stage whisper.

"It's because I know that if I didn't say yes, Cassie would do it anyway, and she'd get Rachel to go along, and possibly you, and the three of you need someone . . . someone sensible along."

"Yes, *Dad*," I mocked.

Jake made this deep-in-the-throat grinding

noise he makes sometimes. But I just laughed. Jake's been my best friend forever. He may be leader of the Animorphs, but that doesn't mean I have to take him too seriously.

We followed the woman and the parrots up to the point when she walked through a doorway into a storage room. We waited till she came back out and headed up to clean the parrot perch. Then into the storage room we went.

"Dee dee dee, dee dee dee, dee dee dee, da dum!" I hummed.

"Have I mentioned shut up, Marco?" Rachel asked me in a conversational tone.

"Okay, come on, you guys," Cassie urged.

We went to the parrot cage. Cassie removed the birds one by one, placing them into our hands. The birds remained very quiet as we acquired them.

That's what we call it when we absorb the DNA of an animal: acquiring. It always puts the animal in a kind of trance. The parrots were no different.

We hid the parrots in a well-ventilated cupboard. Cassie assured us it was safe. And now all that was left to do was to become the parrots. To morph the parrots.

So that's what we did.

CHAPTER 2

Most people would think morphing into an animal is fun. And I guess it is. But what it is, more than fun, is terrifying. And bizarre. And extreme.

Until you've done it, it's impossible to really understand how extreme it is.

The body you've had since you were born, the body with two arms and two legs and a head with your own personal face stuck on the front, changes. It changes completely. Until nothing is left of you but your mind. You don't have your fingers to wiggle, or your legs to stand on, or your mouth to talk with. You look at the world through another animal's eyes.

As I focused my mind on the parrot, I felt the

changes begin. The first thing that happened was that my skin turned green.

Not that tinge of green you might get when you're sick or something. I'm talking GREEN. Brilliant, glowing, lustrous green. The green of the parrot's feathers.

"Whoa! Cool!" I said.

And it was cool, because at that same moment, the others were changing colors, too. Jake was turning as white as snow. Dead white. Rachel was a fascinating mix of yellow and orange. And Cassie . . . well, Cassie has a sort of unconscious talent for morphing. On her, deep crimson, red the color of blood, spread down from her shoulders, down and down her arms, down to her fingertips. Then the color rose up her neck, to change her face like it was a glass pitcher being slowly filled with cherry Kool-Aid. The very last things to change were the whites of her eyes. For a brief second they shone white, then, like all the rest of her, they turned red.

Once my entire body was brilliant green, I began to shrink. The dirty floor of the storeroom rose up to meet me. It was like I was falling. Like I'd passed out and was dropping facefirst toward the floor.

And as I shrank, my feet became bird feet. My thick, solid human bones became hollow bird bones. My internal organs, my lungs and stomach and liver, all twisted around in ways that should have made me scream in agony — except for the fact that morphing technology deadens pain.

My green skin became even brighter as I became smaller. Feather patterns drew themselves across my skin. My fingers sprouted outward and thinned to become feathers.

And then my face simply exploded outward. My *entire* face. Just, SPROOT! My teeth, my lips, my nose, my chin, all bulged out like they were made of Silly Putty and someone was sticking their fist through from behind.

My skin — the skin that had been my cheeks and lips — turned hard. Hard as old fingernails. My huge, ridiculously large parrot beak was forming. It was the color of old-man fingernails.

I looked out at my friends through sharply focused eyes. Not quite hawk eyes, but better than human vision.

<Well, aren't we colorful?> I said in thought-speak. Thought-speak is the telepathy we have when we're in morph.

<Better get into the cage quick, before that woman comes back,> Cassie urged.

And right about then, I felt the parrot brain bubble up within my own human mind. It was weird. I've dealt with animal brains that were nothing but fear, like a mouse brain, and animal brains that were all about killing, like a wolf spider's brain. I've even had to deal with the machinelike, soulless brain of the ant. But it is rare to actually feel something like intelligence in that animal brain.

I've been a gorilla and a dolphin, and both of those are very smart animals. The parrot wasn't that smart, but there was definite thinking power in that brain. The parrot could think. It could reason. And, I realized, it could feel. It could feel emotions beyond simple instinct.

The parrot brain didn't overwhelm my human consciousness. It was just there. And as I began to realize how complex that brain was, I began to understand why Cassie was so mad.

<Hey. These birds are smart,> I said.

<Very smart,> Cassie agreed. <Too smart to be stuck out there on a crappy perch and be pestered all day. These birds should be flying free in the rain forest, not stuck in a mall.>

<Not that we can really run around freeing every parrot in the country,> Jake said pointedly. <We're clear on that, right?>

<Yeah, but we can make the Amazon Cafe wish it never heard of parrots,> I said.

A few minutes later, the woman came to carry us back out to the clean perches. I looked around at the crowd gathered there.

<Ah, so many people, so little time to insult

them all,> I said. Then I tried something I have never tried with any morph. I tried to make the parrot speak.

Here's a clue: It's not easy talking when you have no lips. All the sounds have to kind of be made in the throat. Like a ventriloquist. But I figured it out. We all did. And then there was nothing left for us to do but talk to all the people standing in line.

And talk is what we did.

"Squuuuaaaakkk! Amazon burgers are made with cat meat! Squuuaaaakkk!"

"Squuuaaaakkk! Try our spaghetti with hair!"

"Squuuaaaakkk! Amazon Cafe nachos and toe jam!"

Tobias was in the crowd smirking as he watched the people turn slightly green. Ax was with him, scarfing a slice of pizza he'd gotten somewhere. I could only hope it wasn't from the trash.

"Squuuaaakkk! Botulism! Food poisoning!"

"Squuuaaakkk! Enjoy the fried booger strips!"

Oddly enough, many people standing in line decided to go and find another restaurant. The restaurant manager took about five minutes to decide that real-live parrots were maybe *not* a good idea. But we decided we'd make dead sure he got the message.

"Squuaaaakkk! By the way, is that your nose or are you eating a banana?"

"Squuaaakkk! What's that on your head, a wombat?"

"Squuaaakkkk! It's a toupee! It's a toupee! Squuaaakkk!"

"Squuaaakkk! We should be flying free in our native habitat!"

That last one was Cassie, of course. It was a little talky for a parrot, if you asked me.

After that we were outta there. I spotted Tobias applauding softly and laughing. I was feeling pretty good, pretty cocky. Until I saw another face behind Tobias, way back in the crowd.

I knew the face. Erek.

Erek, the Chee.

CHAPTER 3

Erek the Chee used to be Erek this guy I knew from school. But Erek is a lot more than just some guy.

The Chee are a race of androids. They pass as humans by projecting a sort of holographic energy field around themselves that looks human. Erek may look like a kid. But he is older than human history.

The Chee came to Earth hundreds of thousands of years ago. They were companions to the Pemalites, whose home planet had been devastated by a violent invasion. The Pemalites had fled, but too late. By the time they reached Earth, the Pemalites were finished.

Their deathless androids did all they could.

They gave the essence of the Pemalites a new life. They melded them with wolves. And from this union dogs were born.

If you know how basically sweet and faithful and loving dogs are, you know what the Pemalites were like. And you also know a little of what the Chee are like.

The Chee are peaceful, but not out of weakness. Erek, all by himself, could have taken on every person in the mall that day, beaten them all, and ripped the mall down around our ears. Literally.

But the Chee are pacifists. It's the way they are. They are also enemies of the Yeerks. They watch the Yeerks and learn about them, and, in their nonviolent way, do all they can to delay the Yeerks.

Erek waited till we were done with our little prank. He waited till I was walking away through the mall with Jake. We had split from the others so as not to look like a "group."

"Hi, Marco," Erek said. "Hello, Jake."

We didn't exactly rush over to throw our arms around him. We'd seen what happened the one time Erek did go postal. It was hard to forget. Hard to treat someone that powerful like just another kid.

"Hi, Erek, how's it going?" Jake asked guardedly.

"Fine. And we know, through our sources, that you have been doing good work against . . . against our mutual acquaintances." He lowered his voice. "I think we'd better have some privacy."

Suddenly, the air around us shimmered. All the noises of the mall were blanked out. And Erek was no longer human. He was a chrome-and-ivory robot, shaped a little like a lean dog, walking erect.

"What did you do?" I asked.

"I extended my hologram out around us all. People walking by are seeing a group of security guards talking. No one will bother or overhear us."

It was a cool trick. But it made my stomach do a little flip. Erek wasn't going to all this trouble just to talk about sports or whatever.

"Rescuing the two free Hork-Bajir was a good thing. They may prove to be the seeds of something very powerful and good. You may have begun the salvation of an entire race."

I shrugged. "We like to keep busy. It's either rescue entire races or play Nintendo."

Erek laughed with his chrome dog's muzzle. Then he was instantly serious again. "I need to talk to you privately, Marco."

"Well, I don't have any secrets from Jake," I

said. "I think that's the basis of a good marriage: openness, honesty."

"It's about someone who was once very close to you, Marco."

My heart stopped beating. I knew instantly who he meant. I started to say something, but my first words died on my tongue. I tried again. "My mom?"

Erek glanced at Jake.

"It's okay," Jake said. "I know. I'm the only one who does."

Erek nodded. "Marco, your mother has returned to Earth. She is overseeing some very secret new project. It's being run from Royan Island. Or, to be precise, it's being run from the waters around Royan Island."

I wasn't really hearing what Erek was saying. I was still back on the part about my mom returning to Earth. Jake understood. He took over dealing with Erek.

"What are they doing out there in the ocean?"

"We don't know," Erek said. "But whatever it is, it would have to be huge for Visser One to be overseeing it."

"Visser Three must be a little ticked about that."

Erek nodded. "Visser Three is not one of Visser One's favorite Yeerks. And vice versa."

"Yeah," Jake agreed.

"Look, I . . . we weren't sure whether to tell you about this. But we've learned all we can. And I felt Marco had a right to know she was back on Earth. But you guys have to be clear about something. Visser One didn't get to the top of the Yeerk hierarchy by being nice. She is brilliant and dangerous."

Jake looked at me to see how I was reacting.

"You guys think I don't know what Visser One is like?!" I said hotly.

"I know you do," Erek said. "But humans are easily tricked by outer appearances. You judge people by their faces and eyes. The face of Visser One is the face of someone you trust, Marco. But if you Animorphs decide to investigate this thing on Royan Island, you may come up against Visser One directly."

I could see where he was going. And it made me mad. I don't even know why. "Look, Erek, I'm not an idiot, okay?"

He shook his robot head. "I know you aren't. But you love your mother. You want to save her. So you may make mistakes."

I swear I would have swung at Erek. But he would have let me hit him. And I would have just hurt my hand.

"There's one other clue," Erek said. "We have

19

reason to believe that some new species of Controller is at Royan Island. We believe they are called Leerans."

"Thanks, Erek," Jake said.

"Will he be all right?" Erek asked Jake.

I didn't wait to hear Jake's answer. I turned and stepped out of the hologram. I saw a woman's eyes widen in shock. What she had seen was a kid stepping directly out of a casually chatting security guard.

Jake caught up with me a few seconds later.

"Erek didn't mean anything bad. You know that," Jake said. "He just meant —"

"I know what he meant," I snapped. "He meant if it came to crunch time, would I destroy my own mother to protect the mission? That's what he meant."

Jake grabbed my shoulder and turned me around. "And?"

I was still mad. But I knew why I was mad. It wasn't that Erek had insulted me somehow. It was that Erek was right.

"I don't know, Jake," I said. "I don't know."

CHAPTER 4

<Yes, I know what a Leeran is. I have heard of that species,> Ax said. <But where did you hear that word?>

It was the next day after school, out in the woods where Ax and Tobias lived. Tobias was off hunting. I wanted to talk to Ax alone. He was in his own body, of course, watching me with his main eyes while his stalk eyes cautiously scanned the trees in every direction.

I had asked Jake not to say anything to the others about Erek. The others didn't know that Visser One was my mother. They all thought what I had thought for the past two years. That my mom had drowned. That her body had never been found.

I hadn't wanted the others to know the truth. That my mother had been made into a Controller. That the Yeerk inside her head was the original commander of the Earth invasion.

I didn't want their pity. I still don't. I'm a joker. I'm a comedian. That's how I deal with life. See, I've always believed that to some extent you get to decide for yourself what your life will be like. You can either look at the world and say, "Oh, isn't it all so tragic, so grim, so awful." Or you can look at the world and decide that it's mostly funny.

If you step back far enough from the details, everything gets funny. You say war is tragic. I say, isn't it crazy the way people will fight over nothing? People fight wars to control crappy little patches of empty desert, for crying out loud. It's like fighting over an empty soda can. It's not so much tragic as it is ridiculous. Asinine! Stupid!

You say, isn't it terrible about global warming? And I say, no, it's funny. We're going to bring on global warming because we ran too many leaky air conditioners? We used too much spray deodorant, so now we'll be doomed to sweat forever? That's not sad. That's irony.

Note to Alanis: *That* is ironic.

But humor kind of breaks down when the tragedy gets up close and personal.

See, I saw what my mom's "death" did to my

dad. And you know what? There wasn't anything funny about it. And I know that for a year I cried myself to sleep most nights, looking at her picture. I still feel like someone blew a hole in me. A hole that will never heal. A hole I don't *want* to heal, because I don't *want* to stop hurting for my mom, I don't *want* to get over it.

Jake knew my mom. So when we all came face-to-face with Visser One, he knew who she was. But not Rachel or Cassie or Tobias or Ax. And since we'd been in animal morph at the time, the human-Controller known as Visser One did not recognize "her" son.

<Where did you hear about Leerans?> Ax asked me again.

"Look, can you just tell me what you know about them?"

Ax hesitated. He is still a little uncomfortable being open and honest with humans. The Andalites are not used to trusting other species.

<They are an aquatic race. Their planet is mostly water, like Earth. Only their land masses don't have much life. The most advanced life-forms are in the oceans. The Leerans are a sentient race of amphibians.> He shrugged. <At least, that's what I learned in school. I've never met a Leeran, of course. They aren't allowed on our world.>

"Not allowed? Why not? Are they dangerous?"

Ax laughed. He gets this kind of superior, know-it-all attitude sometimes. <Of course not *dangerous.* More like embarrassing.>

"Why? Do they fart in public or something?"

<Leerans are supposed to be psychic. They can read minds. At least they can do it if they're within close range. We have technological and military secrets we don't want the Leerans to know. Plus, you know, thoughts you might not want strangers listening in on. Now, where did you hear about Leerans?>

"Erek. The Chee. He says there's some kind of secret underwater thing going on with the Yeerks. He says some Leerans are involved."

Ax looked puzzled. <Yeerks and Leerans? It doesn't make sense. The Yeerks could never invade the Leeran world like they're doing with Earth. The Leerans are psychic. They would instantly know if one of their people were a Controller.>

"Yeah. You're right. On the other hand . . . if you *could* make Controllers out of these Leerans. Psychic Controllers?"

Ax swiveled his stalk eyes toward me. <They would be able to root out spies. Like the Chee. They would be able to sense traitors.>

"And they would be able to find five human kids and one Andalite," I said. "They would see right through an animal morph. They would mean the end of us."

I took a deep breath and let it out slowly. Through a gap in the trees I spotted a hawk soaring just over the treetops. Maybe Tobias, maybe not. In addition to fantastic sight, hawks have excellent hearing. I wondered, if it was Tobias, if he'd overheard my conversation with Ax.

"I guess it doesn't matter," I muttered.

<What doesn't matter?>

"Anything," I said with a laugh. "It doesn't matter, does it?" I guess I always knew my secret would come out sooner or later. Funny-boy Marco is destined to look pathetic. My friends will look at me and think, *Poor, poor Marco.* I shook my head. "Never fails, you know. The Irony Gods. They wait for the chance to twist your life around. Mr. Cool-and-Detached ends up being the object of pity. Great. Perfect."

<These Irony Gods are a human religion?> Naturally Ax was totally mystified by my babbling.

"No. They're just a Marco religion," I said. "The Irony Gods wait to find out whatever it is you *don't* want. And that's what they do to you."

<And this is funny?> Ax asked. He's a little unsure of human humor.

"Absolutely," I said. "If it was happening to someone else, it would be hysterical."

CHAPTER 5

In the end I told Jake we *had* to do it. We had to find out what the Yeerks were doing on Royan Island.

But I told him not to tell the others the rest of it. About my mom. I still hoped somehow we'd be able to avoid my dark secret. And avoid pity.

"Royan Island is a small, private island about twenty miles off the coast," I told the others when we were assembled in Cassie's barn. The barn is also the Wildlife Rehabilitation Clinic. The place where Cassie and her dad take in injured or sick wild animals.

It was Saturday morning. We were planning to take a first, casual look at Royan Island.

"It's about four miles long and three miles wide and shaped like a crescent moon," I continued.

"Very poetic," Rachel said. "Crescent moon."

"Hey, it's a quote from the guidebook, all right?!" I said. I winced. I shouldn't have snapped like that. I should have had a comeback ready. I looked tense, snapping at Rachel.

I took a deep breath. "Anyway, Ax says these Leerans are psychic. So we have to be very careful. We can't get near one of them."

"How near is near?" Jake asked Ax.

<I don't know,> Ax admitted. <I think a few feet. But I don't know.>

"How do we get to the island?" Cassie wondered. "By air or by sea?"

<Twenty miles is a long way to try and swim,> Tobias pointed out. He was up in the rafters, as usual. Keeping an eye out through the open loft and listening with his hawk hearing.

"So we do a combination," Jake said. "Fly out there. Rest. Morph to dolphin."

<Not everyone has a dolphin morph,> Tobias pointed out. <I can fly cover.>

I saw Cassie cock an eyebrow at Tobias. I think we were having the same thought. It was a little like Tobias didn't want to morph, now that he had his morphing power back.

"Ax has a shark morph from when we first rescued him," I said. "That will do as well as dolphin. And if Tobias doesn't want to morph —"

<I didn't say that,> Tobias said quickly.

Jake looked at his watch. "Tobias, you could still fly out to The Gardens and acquire a dolphin morph. The Gardens are on the way, more or less."

<I have to remain in my own body to acquire a morph,> Tobias pointed out. <Kind of obvious, a red-tailed hawk suddenly landing on a dolphin.>

"Yeah. Well. Never mind, then," Jake said. "Come as you are." He smiled. "You've always been our secret weapon just the way you are."

Tobias hesitated. <No, you're right. I should do the dolphin thing. Twenty miles over water . . . those aren't really my best flying conditions. You tend not to get thermals over water. I'll do it. I'll acquire a dolphin morph. Okay. I'll definitely do it. And then, hey, no problem. Right? I mean, a dolphin in water, that's like a bird in the air, right?>

We were all staring at him. Tobias isn't usually a babbler. But he was babbling. It was Cassie who figured it out first.

"Tobias? Are you afraid of water?"

<Water? Afraid? Me?>

"I'd say that's a yes." I laughed. "You're not afraid to be a mile up in the air, but you're afraid of water?"

<Not water,> he said hotly. <It's just that, you know, there's no air in the water. You can't breathe. It presses in all around you.>

"Hey, how about if we stop busting on Tobias, okay?" Rachel growled. "If he doesn't like water, he doesn't have to like water."

<No, it's okay,> Tobias said shakily. <I'm cool. I mean, I'll be a dolphin, right? They live in the water.>

I nodded. "Yep. We've established that dolphins live in water."

"Okay, then," Jake said. "Tobias needs to go to The Gardens to play with the dolphins. And we need to make this fast. So let's fly, and let's hope we get lucky."

<They hold their breath underwater, right?> Tobias asked. <I mean, I guess that's obvious. But if they ever forgot . . . >

"It'll be okay," Cassie reassured him. "You'll see. Once you've been a dolphin, you'll never fear the ocean again."

<The ocean. Oh, man. The entire ocean.>

I don't know why, but Tobias being scared made me feel better. I guess it's true that misery loves company.

"Let's morph," Jake said.

And a few minutes later, I had curved, swept-back wings, brilliant white feathers, and a serious passion for garbage.

CHAPTER 6

If you want to fly high and far, take on a bird-of-prey morph. But if you want to be able to go anywhere, without anyone really noticing, be a seagull.

Seagulls and pigeons can appear anywhere and do anything without anyone getting upset. But if you show up as a bald eagle, people are going to notice.

We'd all done seagull morphs before, except for Tobias and Ax. We figured Tobias had enough to deal with having to acquire a dolphin, so no one suggested he do a gull, too. But Ax is a different story. Cassie had an injured seagull in her barn. So Ax had quickly acquired it.

We flew to The Gardens swift and low, the way

seagulls do. And we noticed every last piece of edible garbage on the way. Every stray french fry, bread crust, burger fragment, candy wrapper, cheese puff, and melted jujube. Seagulls are as good at spotting edible garbage as hawks are at spotting mice.

<I cannot believe I'm flying with seagulls,> Tobias sneered. <I could get kicked out of the hawk fraternity for hanging out with lowlifes.>

Actually, Tobias wasn't exactly hanging out with us. He was flying higher, about two hundred feet above us. But Tobias has been a hawk so long he relates almost as much to other birds as he does to humans. He respects and fears golden eagles and falcons, both of which will occasionally attack a hawk. But he actively dislikes pigeons, seagulls, and above all, crows. I think it's something to do with the groupy nature of those birds. Tobias is a loner.

I spotted The Gardens up ahead. It was easy, since the roller coaster is about ten stories high. And I saw lots of other gulls circling in the sky over the amusement park and zoo.

<Ah, our brothers and sisters await,> I said.

<They probably already got all the good food,> Rachel grumbled.

She was joking. I hoped.

We swept on a following breeze above the parking lots and above the fences and right over

31

the gate where we would have had to pay if we'd been human.

<Let's go this way!> I yelled, suddenly excited. I've always loved amusement parks. I live for coasters. Or at least I did before I became an Animorph and discovered bigger thrills.

<Which way?> Jake asked.

<This way!> I banked my wings and suddenly shot left. Straight for the wooden roller coaster. A car was clank-clank-clanking its way up the first main hill. I flapped my wings and swooped right for it.

The first car had two guys in it. Not much different than Jake and me, I guess. They were holding their arms up in the air, getting that anticipation rush.

I flew straight for them and landed on the front railing of the car at the moment it reached the top of the hill.

"Whoa. Birds!"

<Marco, what are you doing?> Jake asked. <We're not here to play around.>

But he landed right beside me. Jake has gotten awfully responsible lately. But he's still my old bud.

"Get away, birds!" one of the kids said.

We ignored him, and just then, the coaster dipped over the top of the hill. Down we went.

Down and down, faster and faster. I clutched the railing with all the strength in my seagull feet.

<Yaaaahh!> I yelled.

"Whoa-oh-oh!" the kids shouted.

The bottom of the hill rushed up at us. Down we shot. Then the bottom and up, up, up at a hundred miles an hour, and right then, at maximum speed, I opened my wings. The car dropped out from under me and I was airborne again.

<Yee-HAH!> I yelled.

<You're nuts!> Jake cried, but he followed my lead. The two of us blasted off like we'd been shot out of a cannon.

<Look out!> Whitewashed wooden beams were dead ahead, the supports for the coaster. I trimmed my wings, turned on my side, and blew through a gap in the timbers with no more than two inches of clearance all around.

<Come on. Now that was cool, admit it!> I told Jake.

<Yeah. That was cool.>

<We're still our old selves, aren't we? I mean, we haven't changed. Not really. No matter what, right?>

<Sure, Marco.>

<No, I mean it.> I realized I had grown very serious. I don't know why, but I wanted Jake to agree with me. It was important to me. <We're

still just us. Nothing that happens can really change what you are. Right?>

We flapped side-by-side back to the others.

<Look, Marco,> Jake said wearily. <I'm not exactly a philosopher, okay?>

<Yeah. Well, I'm me, no matter what,> I said defiantly. <No matter how many morphs, no matter how many battles. No matter what. I'll still be me. Everyone better accept that.>

Jake laughed a little. <Marco, if it makes you feel any better, you'll always just be a punk to me.>

I had to laugh, too. <Thanks,> I said.

We flew over to the dolphin tank. Smooth gray torpedoes were swimming patterns against a blue background.

<This ought to be interesting,> I said. <A hawk making physical contact with a dolphin?>

I didn't know just how right I was.

CHAPTER 7

I guess we hadn't really thought it through too well. See, as humans all we had to do to "acquire" a dolphin was to pet it as it came up to the side of the dolphin tank.

But Tobias in his normal hawk body does not have hands. He has talons. And if you've ever looked at hawk talons, you know they are weapons as much as they are feet. Hawks hunt with their talons, not their beaks.

Jake and I saw Tobias circling high overhead. He was hesitating.

<Might as well get it over with,> I called up cheerfully. I was still kind of powered up from the stunt on the roller coaster.

<Fine,> Tobias said grimly.

He wheeled, spilled the air from his wings, and down he came. Down like a bullet.

Now, I should mention that this was a Saturday. It was early still, so the place wasn't full, but there were plenty of people around. The dolphin pool was ringed with people in the bleachers and pressed up close to the pool.

But no one was watching the sky. Except for one little kid. One little kid, who pointed upward and in a clear voice that somehow penetrated above all the background noise said, "Mommy! That bird is going to hurt the dolphins!"

"Tseeeeeer!" Tobias screamed in his best red-tailed way.

<Um . . . is this stupid?> Cassie asked, way too late.

One of the dolphins shot up out of the water, clear up and out. And Tobias went for him.

"Ooooh!" the crowd gasped.

And Tobias struck. Like he was going after a mouse. Only this was a really big mouse.

Talons raked forward, wings flared to act as air brakes, Tobias struck. And then, he *stuck*.

Talons sank into smooth, rubbery dolphin flesh while the dolphin was still arcing through the air. It was a weird aerial ballet: the huge dolphin and the tiny hawk, colliding ten feet above the water. It would have been beautiful if it hadn't been insane.

"Aaaahhhh!" the crowd murmured.

Down went the dolphin.

<Oh, man, I'm stuck!> Tobias cried. <My left talon is —>

And then he stopped thought-speaking because the dolphin had fallen back into the water. And Tobias had gone with him.

Pah-LOOOSH!

A huge splash. And now the crowd was on its feet.

"Whoa!"

"Is that part of the show?" someone said.

"No way. Look at the dolphin trainers. They're going nuts!"

This was true. The trainers were going ape. They were racing around the pool trying to get the dolphin's attention, hoping to get it to pull over and let them grab the lunatic bird.

But dolphins like to play. And this was a whole new cool game. I guess Tobias wasn't hurting the dolphin, because the dolphin just grinned his perpetual grin and went tearing through the water.

Up. Down. Up. Down. Flying high, crashing deep. And all the while Tobias kept yelling.

<Aaaahhhh! He's gonna drown me!>

37

We all yelled helpful advice.

<Hold your breath!>

<Gee, really?! Do you think?! Hold my breath?!> Tobias managed to respond.

<He must be okay,> I said. <He's still capable of being sarcastic.>

<Let go!> Ax advised.

<Why didn't I think of that?> Tobias answered. <Ahhhh!>

<Start acquiring him!> Rachel said. <It will put him in a trance.>

<I am acquiring him,> Tobias said. <Guess what? He's not in a trance. Ahhhhh!>

<I'm going to help,> I said.

<How?> Jake asked.

<Kamikaze!>

I aimed for where I thought Tobias would surface next. I spilled air from my wings, trimmed my tail, and dived.

Suddenly, the dolphin leaped clear of the water. He leaped, in fact, straight toward a hoop that was suspended over the water. It was easy to see that the dolphin would glide effortlessly through the circle. And it was just as easy to see that the hawk on his back would not fit.

<Oh. No,> Tobias said matter-of-factly.

I rocketed down, a white blur. Tobias was a target, swooping through the air on the back of the dolphin. I made a last-second adjustment with my tail and . . .

BONK! I hit Tobias hard, knocking him clear of the dolphin. The dolphin shot through the hoop.

<Ow!> Tobias yelled.

<Ow, yourself, I just saved your life,> I said.

Tobias flapped his sodden wings and labored for altitude. <Thanks. Next time find a way to save me that doesn't involve breaking any bones.>

CHAPTER 8

We flew from The Gardens out toward the ocean. Everyone was in a pretty good mood, with the possible exception of Tobias.

<The dolphin looked okay,> Cassie said. <Very superficial cuts. The vets will put some salve on him and give him a preventive antibiotic, I suppose, just to be careful.>

<Well, as long as the *dolphin* is okay,> Tobias said. <Because I really, really hope the *dolphin* is okay.>

<Are you going to be sarcastic the rest of the day?> I asked him.

<Yes. I am going to be sarcastic the rest of the day. I nearly drowned. Now I'm going to go

become the thing that nearly drowned me. I will be sarcastic until further notice.>

I guess it's dumb, but, once again, I was kind of glad Tobias was in a bad mood. It distracted me from my own thoughts. If I could keep busy teasing Tobias, I didn't have to think about the fact that I was flying closer to where my mother was.

<You know,> I said thoughtfully, <that could be a regular act at The Gardens. Hawk and dolphin. Kind of a dolphin rodeo, if you really think about it.>

<Hey, Marco? You need to remember that you're just a lowly seagull right now, which is practically a pigeon, and I'm a hawk,> Tobias said. <You want to keep grinding my nerves, I'll be glad to show you the difference when it comes to aerial combat.>

<Dolphin rodeo. I'm just saying it has possibilities.>

We flew across the beach and the surfline and out over sparkling blue water. It was a warm day and the water was calm. We weren't getting the kind of big, plump thermals Tobias liked for flying, but we weren't dealing with totally dead air, either.

Almost immediately, we spotted Royan Island. It was a dark, lumpy silhouette on the hori-

zon. It took another thirty minutes of hard flying to reach the island.

There wasn't much of a beach there, which I guess is why the island had never become a tourist destination. It was pine trees gnarled by exposure to ocean winds, and tall grass with sprinkles of wildflowers. At one end of the island was a mansion surrounded by smaller buildings. A dock extended out into a small, protected inlet. There was a bloated motor yacht moored there. Behind it was a sleek, fast cigarette boat.

<So that's Mr. Royan's house, I guess?> Rachel asked.

<No. The original Royan was a bootlegger back in the twenties. According to the guidebook, the house is owned by the Marquez family now. Whoever they are.>

<Let's land as far from the house as we can get,> Jake said.

We landed in a stand of trees that lined a driftwood-strewn beach. I saw a couple of old beer cans and soda cans covered by grass. It didn't look like anyone had been there recently.

We all came out of morph. All except Tobias, who stayed up to fly cover.

<There are people in the house,> he reported. <A guard posted on the roof. Another guard down at the dock. Both are carrying concealed weapons.>

He flew back to rejoin us. He landed on a rotting driftwood log and began preening his feathers.

"Very useful, having your hawk's eyes," I said.

<Don't try to make up,> he said, but not angrily. <Dolphin rodeo, huh?>

"Guards don't mean anything," Rachel said. "Whoever owns that house is mega-rich. They can afford to be careful."

"According to Erek, what we're looking for is underwater," Jake said. "May as well get going. See what is down there. If anything."

"Okay. Let's morph. Everyone to dolphin. Except Ax, of course, who will be doing his shark morph." Jake looked at Ax. Then at Ax's hooves. "We need to get rid of those hoof marks in the sand. A Yeerk might possibly recognize them as Andalite."

<Yes, Prince Jake.>

"Just Jake," Jake said tolerantly.

We waded out into the water till we were up to our waists. It was cold. I felt sand rush between my toes, pulled by the current. Tobias came down and landed on Rachel's shoulder.

"Let's do it," Rachel said impatiently.

"Let's get fishical, fishical," I sang.

Rachel groaned. "Olivia Newton-John? Have you been listening to dinosaur-rock radio again?"

"How about you? You actually know who sang that song."

"My mom controls the radio in the car," Rachel said with a shudder. "And she wonders why I don't go places with her."

"Is there any chance we could just do what we came here to do?" Jake asked impatiently.

"Anyway, dolphins aren't fish," Cassie said. "Mammals."

<Oh, everyone shut up and let's get this over with!> Tobias yelled.

I winked at Cassie. "Tense. Very tense. Too many high-caffeine mice."

I had morphed dolphin before, so I knew what to expect. But even knowing what to expect doesn't keep morphing from being extremely weird.

I focused my mind on the dolphin. And almost immediately I lost my legs. They seemed to be stuck together. As if someone had Krazy-Glued my thighs and calves. I waved my arms wildly, trying to keep my balance. But then my feet began to wither up and it was all over.

SPLASH! I went down, facefirst, into the water. I opened my eyes underwater and looked back at my body. Like I said, every morph is different. And for some reason, this time I was morphing from my feet upward. The lower half of my body was already almost pure dolphin.

"Good grief, I'm a mermaid!" I said. Although since I was trying to talk underwater, all anyone else heard was "Bloop bleep bloym bl blomblay!"

What had been my feet had become a furled scroll of gray rubber. As I watched, the scroll unfurled to become a tail. Gray rubber moved up my body like a tide. But it was happening too slowly to keep me from needing air.

With awkward human arms, I windmilled my arms to bring my head above water. As I did, I noticed the bizarre sight of a red-tailed hawk with its feathers melting into gray skin. As Tobias's beak suddenly expanded outward into a dolphin snout, I slipped back under the water.

My arms were shriveling. My fingers stuck together, then grew a sheath of the same gray rubber flesh to form a flipper.

I felt a little tingle at the back of my neck and realized that as I lay facedown in the sea, I could breathe through my newly formed blowhole.

Suddenly, my eyes changed and the silty, stinging saltwater became clearer, almost like swimming pool water. I could see the others. They were almost totally dolphin. Only here and there were a few lingering bits of humanness. Jake's flippers still had pink fingers sticking out of them. Cassie still had a human mouth. As I watched, it bulged out and split into the usual toothy dolphin grin. Of course, Tobias didn't show lingering humanity. His last fading traces were pure red-tail: He had reddish feathers sticking out of his dolphin tail.

But within seconds those final traces were gone and we were a normal pod of dolphins. All except Ax, that is.

We had rescued Ax from the submerged Dome of the wrecked Dome ship. He'd been down there for a while, so he'd acquired a morph that seemed useful to him. The morph of a shark.

I felt the dolphin consciousness bubbling up within my own. Dolphins are just about the coolest animal minds I've ever experienced. They may be the original party animals. Life is one big game to them. They like to eat fish, and they like to play.

But man, they do not like sharks.

And neither did I. See, the first time I went into dolphin morph, a shark cut me almost in two. And that kind of thing will stick with you, you know?

It's Ax, I told myself. *Not a tiger shark, just Ax.*

But he looked at me with those dead, blank shark's eyes, and I couldn't help but feel a chill, despite my dolphin playfulness.

CHAPTER 9

<Let's just swim a circle around this island and see what we see,> Jake suggested.

<I'm guessing what we'll see is fish,> I said. <The more I think about this, the more I wonder if maybe Erek was wrong. This island looks awfully peaceful.>

<I don't think the Chee make many mistakes,> Cassie said. <But look, why waste time worrying about it? Let's swim!>

Cassie took off at high speed through the water, and I couldn't help but give chase. Soon the five of us were tearing around at maximum dolphin warp, leaping out of the waves, diving to the bottom only to go ripping back for the surface, and just generally behaving like happy five-year-olds.

It was a party in the water. The water felt warm now. Warm and slick as it rushed across my smooth skin. I dove deep, holding my breath for long minutes. I skimmed just inches above the sandy bottom, then rolled over and looked up at the sun, a distant, wobbling yellow ball that jumped this way and that through the water distortion.

I fired a burst of echolocation clicks from my head and got back an amazing "picture" made up of bouncing echoes. My clicks bounced off fish, and off the shoreline, and off the rocks that jutted up from the bottom. The clicks also bounced off Ax, and the picture of his shark body disturbed the perfect happiness of my dolphin mind.

Get over it, I told myself. *He's Ax, not a real shark. Forget sharks. Put sharks out of your mind.*

<Okay, let's focus a little here,> Jake said, trying to impose some order on our idiot play. <Keep the shore to your left and let's take a quick run around the island.>

<You mean like a race?>Tobias asked. <Because that would be cool!>

In my head, I heard Cassie laugh. <So, Tobias. I guess you're past your fear of the water?>

<It's kind of hard to be afraid of anything

48

right now,> he said. <This was worth it. This is so cool. It's like flying, but with a really thick wind. Come on! Race you!>

He took off and the rest of us followed. Ax came up behind us, but he was slower. Maybe his shark brain automatically disliked dolphins as much as dolphins dislike sharks. I don't know. I didn't care. I was in a race!

Down and swim and swim, then up, break the surface to blow out old air and suck in new, then back down to swim and swim, and kick my powerful tail for every iota of speed I could get!

We were zooming madly through the water, each trying to be the fastest around the island.

I hadn't been echolocating for a while but then, as we turned a corner, I fired off a burst. The picture that came back made me stop dead in the water.

<What is *that*?>

<What?> Jake asked.

<Shoot some clicks,> I said.

I heard everyone blasting away, machine-gun bursts of clicks.

<Whoa!>

<What is it?> Ax asked. <Are you sensing something?>

<What is that?> Cassie asked.

<I don't know, but it isn't natural, that's for sure,> Tobias said.

<Let's go see,> I suggested. <There are limits to this echolocation thing.>

We turned away from the island and headed farther out to sea. The thing we had sensed was composed of hard surfaces and sharp edges. And it was huge.

Now our human minds were in charge again. At least mine was. Because I guess I knew this was what Erek had told us about. And if that part of his story was correct, then maybe the rest was, too. Maybe my mother was down there in that place of hard surfaces and sharp edges.

We were in deep water, maybe two hundred feet, when we reached the spot we were looking for. But there was nothing there. Nothing but waving seaweed and jutting rocks and schools of silvery fish.

I fired another echolocating burst. According to my echolocation, there was a massive under-water structure of some sort directly in front of me.

<Erek's trick,> I said. <They're using the same trick the Chee use. It's a hologram. A hologram of a normal seabed. That way divers who may come around won't see it. And it won't be visible to planes flying over on sunny days.>

<Yeah, but is it just a hologram, or a force field like Erek has?> Jake wondered.

<It would take a great deal of energy to sustain a hologram that large,> Ax pointed out. <To maintain a force field in water would take the energy level of a Dome ship.>

<Only one way to find out,> Rachel said. <Let's go.>

We headed straight for the place our eyes told us was just seabed. We swam for maybe fifty feet and then everything changed. It was like sticking your head through a movie screen and suddenly seeing the stage behind it.

There, less than a quarter mile from the mansion on Royan Island and two hundred feet underwater, was a pink-shaded structure built into the side of an underwater slope.

There were three vast openings, each big enough to drive a dump truck through. Two were closed by steel doors. The third was open, revealing a dark tunnel.

Between these large openings were two circular portholes covered by convex glass or plastic. I could see clearly through one of these transparent blisters. Inside there were humans working at computer workstations. It looked weirdly normal. Like any office full of engineers or whatever. A Dilbert-looking place.

Except for the fact that it was in an underwater building.

And of course there was the fact that in Dilbert's world there aren't Hork-Bajir standing guard.

I could see two of the big aliens. Seven feet tall. Blades growing out of their wrists and elbows and knees. Feet like tyrannosaurs. Snakelike heads topped by two or three forward-raked horns. Spike-tipped tails.

Each had a Yeerk in its head. I'd met some free Hork-Bajir. They were kind of sweet, despite their deadly looks. But these were Hork-Bajir-Controllers, of course. And the humans were human-Controllers.

In the second blister window I saw nothing but a single room. In it were a desk and a couple of chairs. And nothing else.

<Okay, so this is the place,> Rachel said. <Now all we have to do is figure out what they're doing here.>

<I need air.> I shot to the surface to blow out and refill my lungs. The others followed. All except Ax, whose gills let him breathe underwater.

We hung around on the surface for a few moments. I wanted to look around and see the normal world, I guess. Feel the air.

<Definitely a Yeerk facility,> Jake said. <I saw Hork-Bajir.>

<I wish I had my own eyes,> Tobias said. <I'd

be able to see what's on those computer monitors inside there.>

<Well, maybe we can just swim around the place a few times,> Cassie suggested. <See if they do anything. I mean, those three big openings are there for some reason. Something is going in and out of that place.>

<Excuse me.>

It was Ax. He was still down under.

<Yeah, Ax, what's up?> Jake asked.

<There are some fish that seem to be heading toward you.>

<Okay. I'm sure it's nothing to worry about.>

But something told me to ask for more details. <Large fish, Ax-man?>

<Yes. As large as my current morph. And they are strange in shape.>

<Strange how?>

<Their heads. They have heads that are flat in the front but extend out on each side. They have eyes at the end of each side extension. Also, they have fins like mine.>

It took a few seconds for me to process that word picture. A large fish with a dorsal fin and a head that . . . My dolphin heart stopped beating.

<Hammerheads!> I yelled. <Hammerheads!>

CHAPTER 10

We drove down beneath the surface, and there they were: hammerhead sharks.

<There must be ten of them!> Tobias said.

<Ten of them against five dolphins and a tiger shark,> Rachel said. <We can handle it.>

There are times when I really admire Rachel's reckless courage. But there are other times when I just want to slap her. We had fought sharks before. We had won, but it had been a close call. Very, very close. And there were more sharks this time.

<Easy, everyone. We don't know they're going to attack us.> Jake said, as calmly as he could with ten sharks heading straight for us.

<Sharks don't usually attack dolphins,> Cassie said. <Not unless they're really hungry and outnumber the dolphins.>

<Well, I count ten of *them* and five of *us*,> I said. <Would that qualify as "outnumbered"?>

<Let's hope they aren't hungry,> Tobias said grimly. <I haven't done this before like you guys. Any tips for fighting sharks?>

<Yeah. Don't let them bite you.>

The sharks came on, straight for us. They came on like well-trained troops. I had a sudden, vivid flash of the searing pain when they'd bitten me once before. They had bitten my dolphin body almost in half. The lower third of me had been left hanging by a few shreds of flesh and some guts.

I have been afraid many times since becoming an Animorph. But this was bad. There are few things as horrifying as watching a shark come at you. Knowing he intends to eat you.

<Okay, look, we don't need this fight,> Jake said. <Let's get out of here.>

<Just run away?!> Rachel asked in outrage.

<You're welcomed to stay behind, Rachel,> I said.

<Hey, we fight Yeerks, not sharks,> Cassie pointed out.

<Exactamundo and I am out of here,> I said.

I kicked my tail and spun around. And that's when I nearly passed out. Nearly died without a single bite being inflicted.

<Oh, my God,> Cassie said. <There are more behind us!>

Four more hammerheads were rushing toward us from behind. Fourteen sharks in all. More than two to one against us.

Jake had already given the order to retreat. But that's not why I did what I did next. What I did next came out of sheer terror.

I ran away.

I powered my tail and took off at right angles to the two groups of sharks.

<Move! Move! Move!> Jake yelled.

But I was already moving. And I didn't even care. I was scared. I could feel those shark's teeth ripping my flesh in my memory. I could feel it like it was happening right now.

I powered away. The others were close behind me, but I was definitely leading the way.

<Head for shore. They may not follow into shallow water,> Cassie said.

The two groups of sharks saw us trying to escape and changed course to cut us off. They were fast. Not as fast as us, maybe, but fast.

The shark groups converged. They were hammer and anvil and we were in between. We raced.

They raced. Too late! Two of the big hammer-heads cut me off.

I turned on a dime. All around us! We were surrounded. Fourteen sets of jaws. Hundreds and hundreds of triangular teeth, each as sharp as a knife.

<Focus on one,> Jake said. <Try to draw blood. The rest will attack whoever is injured.>

It was a good tactic. But I had a feeling about these sharks. Something was very wrong about them.

Jake launched himself at the closest of the monsters. The rest of us followed. Five dolphins and one tiger shark, all churning the saltwater, heading for one unlucky shark.

It happened too fast for the others to react. And I guess the shark we were targeting had gotten cocky. He was too slow to run. Jake slammed the shark with his snout. I was next, ramming the shark with every ounce of momentum I could muster.

WHUMPF!

The impact stunned me, disoriented me. For a few seconds I couldn't see straight. I was aware of the others all hitting the shark in rapid succession. Blood began to billow from the hammer-head's gills. It darkened the water.

<Now's our chance! While they're in a feeding frenzy,> Jake yelled.

But something was wrong. The other sharks didn't attack the wounded one. Blood like a waving silk scarf floated in the water and the sharks ignored it.

Instead, they came after us. It was like they'd had a signal between them. They deliberately moved all at once. They *planned*.

I knew I was going to die. And worst of all, I knew exactly how it would feel.

CHAPTER 11

The injured shark continued spewing blood into the water. The other sharks continued to ignore him.

And the attack was underway!

<We have to break through and run,> Jake said. <Bunch up. Bunch up in a wedge and we'll power our way through.>

We did as he said. We sidled in close together, and on Jake's signal we shot straight ahead. We were one big dolphin fist.

<Don't stop for anything!> Rachel yelled.

But the sharks were already reacting. They had figured out our plan. They were rushing to cut us off. I glanced back and saw that they had left a rear guard just in case we turned around.

Impossible. The sharks were acting together. Like a pack of wolves. And they were plenty smart about it.

<Keep going!> Jake said.

More and more of the sharks had managed to get themselves in front of us. We were closing in on them, and they were closing in on us. I could see individual teeth as they opened their mouths in greedy anticipation of dolphin flesh.

Then I had a flash. A flash of inspiration born out of pure terror.

<Surface!> I yelled.

<What?>

<Sharks don't jump!> I said. <Sharks do not jump.>

Inches from the rows of ripping teeth, we turned and headed up. I rocketed for the surface.

FWOOOSH! Out of the water we came.

PLOOOSH! Down we came. But we came down on the other side of the row of sharks. They turned to chase us, but we had gained several feet on them.

We hauled. The sharks came after us. And unfortunately, we were aimed away from shore out into deep and deeper water.

<Can we outrun them?> Tobias wondered.

<We're about to find out,> I said.

Then . . .

Scree-EEEE-eeee-EEEE-eeee-EEEE-eeee!

It was a siren, just loud enough to be heard with acute dolphin hearing. If I'd been human I doubt I'd have heard it at all. But instantly, without hesitation, the sharks turned around and swam away.

<What was that all about?> Rachel asked.

<Why did they retreat?> Ax wondered, after catching up to the rest of us.

Cassie expressed my own personal feeling at that moment. <Who cares *why*? Let's just get out of here before they change their minds again.>

<Amen,> Tobias said.

But like an idiot I said, <We should go below. See what called them off.> I guess I was starting to realize how it must have looked when I bolted before the others.

<I agree with Marco,> Rachel said.

Naturally, Rachel agreeing with me convinced me I was obviously wrong. But it was too late. We all sucked in a deep lungful of air and went down.

<Yahh! Look out!>

Not twenty feet below us was a submarine. But not a submarine any human ever built. It wasn't all that big, I guess, although it seemed like it when it was right below us. It was shaped like a stingray. It had downcurved water wings on either side. And at the back was a cluster of what looked like three engines, each a twenty-foot-long fattened cylinder, like a comical cigar.

But what was insane about the sub was that about three-quarters of it was perfectly clear. Except for the engines, and occasional tools, implements, and furniture inside, it was a glass submarine.

We could see directly into the sub. I saw three decks, all transparent. It looked like the crew, a mix of human, Hork-Bajir, Taxxon, and Gedd, were all just calmly walking and sitting and standing in the water itself. Plus moving by at a good twenty miles an hour.

At the front of the sub was what had to be the command bridge. There were Hork-Bajir and Taxxons working at red-and-yellow computer terminals. And in the center of the room was a chair. It reminded me of Captain Kirk's chair on the original *Star Trek*.

Standing beside the chair was a bizarre creature. It had pebbly yellowish skin that seemed slimy, like it was coated with Vaseline. It sat like a frog on big hind legs with webbed feet. But instead of a frog's tiny front legs, this creature had four tentacles spaced evenly around its body.

It had a big head that just sat on its shoulders with no neck. The face was curved outward, with a hugely wide mouth that seemed frozen in a sort of idiot grin. There were two eyes, both brilliant green and large.

As the sub passed beneath us, this creature

seemed to shake, like he was having just a slight tremor. I saw him turn around to face us as we receded behind the sub. He gazed at us with his blazing green eyes.

The person sitting in the captain's chair must have said something. Because the frog thing sort of looked troubled, then shrugged in a very humanlike gesture.

The person in the chair stood up. She stretched. She turned around and looked up. Right at us. Right at me.

And I swear I had to stop myself from saying, <Hi, Mom.>

<Visser One!> Rachel said harshly. <So the main creep *is* here on Earth.>

The sub blew past without making a sound. The sharks fell in behind it. And the sub, its occupants, and the sharks all disappeared into the hologram of a nice, normal seabed.

CHAPTER 12

I had homework to do when I got home. Tons of it. I was supposed to do a book report, among other things, and I had to have it in by Monday. Five pages. And my English teacher doesn't respond well to five pages of babble and baloney.

I said hi to my dad. He asked what I wanted to eat for dinner. I said, "Anything but fish."

"Pizza?"

"No anchovies. That's all I'm saying."

I went upstairs and found the book I was supposed to read. It was under a dirty sweatshirt I'd thrown on my desk. I looked at the cover. *Lord of the Rings.* It was three books long and each of the three books was as long as three books. I only had to report on the first book, but even that was impossible.

"What was I thinking, choosing a book this long?" I moaned.

Of course, I knew the answer. I was supposed to have started reading it like a month ago. I flopped down on my bed and placed my head-phones over my ears. Then I pulled a pillow over my head. I fumbled blindly for my remote control and hit PLAY.

Reggae. Some good old classic reggae. Bob Marley. I'd bought the CD at a point when I was considering growing dreadlocks. Never mind why. Okay, it had to do with this girl at school.

"Bob Marley, mon," I said. "Help me out, mon."

Bob didn't help. Bob was singing "No Woman, No Cry." And that translated way too easily in my head into "No Mother, No Cry."

"Great," I muttered. "Let's just wallow in self-pity."

I was not feeling good. No one had called me a coward. Maybe no one had even noticed the way I'd bolted. But I had.

I could come up with great excuses for being so scared. I was the only one who'd ever been chewed almost in half by a shark. And that was a pretty good reason to feel afraid.

But nothing changed the fact that I had run away.

And that feeling was crowded in my head with a whole ton of emotions about seeing my mother.

It was a terrible thing when my mom died. Or at least seemed to die. But as awful as death is, at least there's an end involved. You know what has happened. It makes sense. An awful kind of sense, but sense.

You meet other people who have lost mothers or fathers. You turn on TV and see stories about people who have lost parents or brothers or sisters. You read it in books. In newspapers. The counselors at school have a category for you, and they tell you things that are supposed to help.

You hate it, but you belong to a group of people like yourself.

But what group is there for people whose mother isn't dead but is a slave to an alien presence in her head? What group do I belong to when I realize that what looks like my mother is actually someone who would kill me without hesitation?

I guess it's what Jake feels everytime he sits down to dinner with Tom. I guess he feels the same way I do. Only Jake and I don't talk about that kind of stuff. Jake's my best friend. But he's my best friend because I'm me, you know? Because I'm funny and smart and I'd back him up anytime, any place.

I mean, what am I supposed to do? I'm me, Marco, not some touchy-feely, share-your-feelings-with-the-group kind of person. I don't share feelings, I make people laugh.

I have a picture of my mom next to my bed. I look at it every night before I go to bed. I can never decide what I want to see when I look at it. I don't know if I see the mother I lost, or the mother I want to rescue somehow. I don't know anymore.

I construct little fantasies in my head. Of how I'll get her away from the Yeerks. And I'll keep her locked up for three days until the Yeerk in her head dies from lack of Kandrona rays. And she'll be my mom again.

"And then what, Marco?" I ask myself. The Yeerks won't take it lying down. You can't just starve Visser One to death and take her host body and live happily ever after. We'd be hunted. We'd be hunted for as long as there was a Yeerk left alive on planet Earth.

And if the Yeerks ever did catch up with my mom and dad and me, they'd know I was an Animorph. And then they'd figure it all out and the others would be done for. Jake, Rachel, Cassie, Tobias, Ax . . .

"I am way too young to have to deal with this kind of stuff," I yelled into my pillow. And then I pulled the pillow away from my face.

My dad was standing there, framed in the doorway of my room. He mouthed the words "I knocked." And he did a little pantomime of having knocked.

I yanked the headphones off. "Oh, hi. Um, hi."

"Sorry. I just came to see if you wanted to watch the game with me."

"Oh, yeah. The game," I said. "Um, I guess not. I have homework and stuff."

"Oh. Okay." He started to leave. Then he turned back and said, "You know, Marco, you can always talk to me."

"Oh. Sure, Dad."

"I mean, if there's anything going on that's bothering you."

It was a nice offer. My dad's a nice man. I'd like to grow up to be as good a man as my father. But you know what? Right then, dark suspicion was seeping into my mind. Why was he interested? What did he suspect? Was my father one of them, too?

"Nothing's bothering me, Dad. I was just . . . um, you know, singing along with the music. It was a song lyric."

"Ah. Okay. Well, I'll call up to you when the pizza gets here."

He left, shutting the door behind him.

"Nice world you live in, Marco," I said softly. I could trust my father and maybe end up dead. I could try to help my mother and maybe end up dead. And as a bonus I could get all my friends killed and doom the entire human race.

I looked at the book I was supposed to read. "That ain't happening. Not tonight."

And I thought about my father, sitting down in the living room and turning on the game. Who knew if he was my father any more than my mother was really my mother?

I couldn't really trust him. I couldn't go downstairs and spill all my problems out for him.

But you know what? I could sure go sit with the man and watch the game. I could do that.

CHAPTER 13

"Those were not normal sharks," Cassie pointed out. "Somehow they were being directed. Controlled. They worked like a pack. Sharks don't cooperate."

We had met up in the woods beyond Cassie's farm.

"Are they Controllers? I mean, we discovered horses being made into Controllers," Rachel pointed out.

<No,> Ax said. <Cassie has shown me pictures of the internal structure of a shark. There is no room in that brain for a Yeerk. The structures would never support a Yeerk.>

"Could be implants," I suggested. "You know, electrodes or something."

Everyone just kind of shrugged at that. Who knew? All we knew was that we'd almost been slaughtered by a bunch of very unusual sharks.

<They were guarding that facility, that's clear,> Tobias said.

"All the more reason for us to go in," I said.

Jake kind of raised his eyebrow at me. Rachel nodded agreement. I knew what Jake was thinking. He was thinking I had my own reasons. Reasons only he and I knew about.

I shook my head slightly, telling him no. No, I was not going to tell the others. Not yet. Maybe not ever.

He shrugged and let it go. But I could see he wasn't happy about it.

"I agree we have to go back there," Jake said. "These Leerans Erek talked about. We cannot have some psychic Controllers running around."

"You think that frog-looking thing on the sub was a Leeran?" Cassie asked Ax.

<Yes. Probably.> He sounded uncomfortable. <I haven't exactly memorized the *Encyclopedia of Galactic Life-forms.*>

"Where do you get that encyclopedia?" I asked. "Do they have it at the local library?"

<The question is, what do we do to get a look inside that complex?> Tobias asked.

"You aren't going to like the answer," I muttered.

That got a laugh from everyone.

"We have to think about going hammerhead," Cassie said. "Those guard sharks went after dolphins and Ax's tiger shark. My guess is they go after anything that isn't a hammerhead. And we don't have any hammerheads at The Gardens. However, they do have them at Ocean World. They have a big shark tank. I called over there and found out they do have a big hammerhead. Fourteen feet long."

"Um, excuse me," I said, "but has anyone considered the fact that we all have to be in our own bodies when we acquire one of these sharks?"

I regretted saying it the minute it came out of my mouth. It was like one minute I was all gung ho, and the next minute I was the one weaseling. And after my performance the day before I couldn't afford to be sounding like a weasel.

So I said, "But hey, who's worked up by some little old sharks?"

"You are," Rachel said bluntly.

I felt like she'd kicked me. I mean, maybe she didn't even mean anything by it. But I found myself totally unable to think of a comeback. My cheeks burned. I turned away and pretended to care deeply about some bugs crawling up the trunk of a tree.

"We'd have to go at night," Cassie said.

"Tonight, I guess. And, of course, we have school tomorrow."

"Forget school," I said gruffly. "There's an assembly last period, anyway. We can bail out early and no one will care. Plenty of time to fly out to the island."

Jake nodded. "Okay. Ocean World tonight. The island tomorrow after school. We'll need some good excuses ready for parents in case we run late. I can't get grounded again."

And that was it. Until after sundown that night. I'd told my dad I was going to Jake's house to do homework. I said I might be home a little late. My dad had said to call him if I needed a ride.

We flew to Ocean World and landed in the dark, abandoned park. We demorphed, all of us back to human except Tobias and Ax.

It's funny, because I felt fine being in the dark, abandoned park in my seagull morph. But as a human I felt totally out of place. I felt like I'd get in trouble.

Ocean World is a very new facility. Basically, it's several big fish tanks. Big, as in apartment building size. There is a Plexiglas tunnel you walk through on a slow conveyor belt. The tunnel literally goes through the water. The fish are all around you and even above you.

But we weren't there to be tourists. We

73

couldn't just look at the hammerheads. We had to touch them.

"I wish I knew how we were going to do this," Cassie whispered as she led the way to the shark tank. "Sharks are not dolphins. I mean, these sharks are all well-fed, but they aren't exactly pets."

"Shark-petting. Add that to dolphin rodeo and we have a whole new ESPN show," I said. No one laughed. Jake smirked. But it wasn't a happy kind of smirk.

Personally, I felt like my insides were morphing all on their own. Like my stomach was morphing to some burning liquid.

"I have an idea," Rachel said. "The shark doesn't have to be conscious for us to acquire it, right? So we morph to dolphin. We go into the tank. Six of us against one hammerhead." She shrugged, like we could figure out the rest.

Cassie was shocked. "Just go beat some poor shark half to death? When it's *not* attacking us?"

Rachel held out her hands, being reasonable. "It's a shark, Cassie. A shark. People eat sharks."

"And vice versa," I added.

"Beats just jumping in the pool with it," Jake said. "I mean, in human form how would we even catch a shark?" He looked at Ax. "Or in Andalite form."

Cassie started to say something. But instead she just clenched her jaw tightly, the way she does when she disapproves of something.

"Sharks can *all* die as far as I'm concerned," I said. I laughed like I'd made a joke. But it wasn't a joke.

<They are just predators being predators,> Tobias said. <They aren't evil. Just hungry.>

"So you're on Cassie's side?" I asked him.

<No. Kill or be killed. Eat or be eaten. That's the predator's law. I know. I am a predator. I say we do what we have to do.>

Tobias has toughened up a bit since being trapped in hawk morph.

"Fine," Cassie said tersely. "Let's just get it over with."

We walked toward the fish tanks. They were three wide ovals. Like swimming pools almost. They were built up to make room for the Plexiglas passageways beneath.

There was no sound but our footsteps on concrete. And the sound of Ax's hooves. Nothing to see but deep shadows, made all the darker by the occasional pools of dim light. Nothing to feel but fear.

We were on the pathway to the tanks. Carefully tended bushes lined the walkway. Tobias fluttered along, then dove suddenly.

<Someone's coming!> he said.

We leaped over the bushes. I landed hard on my elbows and rolled under the camouflage of tiny leaves and stiff branches.

Ax leaped, too. But the bushes were only about two feet high. And Ax cannot roll.

A flashlight beam!

"Freeze! Don't move! What the . . ."

I heard the sound of a gun being cocked.

I peered through the bushes and saw a white circle of flashlight beam land squarely on Ax's upper body.

"What on Earth are you? Hey! Hey, Captain! Hey, over here!"

<Prince Jake, what should I do?> Ax asked.

More footsteps. Coming quickly.

"Captain! Look at this! Jeez, will you look at this?"

The first guard kept his beam on Ax. But the beam was shaking, wavering. Not surprising. Ax is not what you'd expect to find on a dark night at a tourist destination aquarium.

The captain aimed a second beam. And I heard a second gun being drawn and cocked.

"What's that?" the captain asked calmly. "Why, that's an Andalite, son. That is certainly an Andalite."

CHAPTER 14

"*A what?*"

"One move, Andalite, and I shoot you. These human weapons may be primitive, but you'd be surprised how effective a lead slug can be."

"Captain, you gotta tell me what's going on here," the first guard said plaintively.

Suddenly . . . WHAP! The captain swung his gun and hit the guard in the side of the head. The guard fell unconscious.

"A tiresome little man," the captain said. "But we'll have one of our people in his brain before he wakes up. Not that it will matter to me. I am off this tiresome detail! For capturing one of the Andalite bandits, I'll be Visser Three's new aide."

<Be careful what you wish for, Yeerk,> Ax sneered. <I've seen the fools who work closely with Visser Three. I've seen their heads go rolling across the ground when the visser gets mad.>

"What do we do?" I asked Jake in a voiceless whisper. His face was just two inches from mine.

"Ax needs a distraction."

It wasn't an order. Or even a suggestion for me to do something. But figured I was better at talking than any of the others. So I stood up on rattling knees.

"Hi. Is this the way to the souvenir stand?" I said cheerfully.

And at the same moment, something fell fast from the sky.

"Tseeeeer!" Tobias screamed. He raked the captain's face with his talons.

"Aarrgghhh!" the guard yelled as he clutched his torn face.

I leaped forward and grabbed the gun. Or tried to.

BOOOM!

The gun erupted. It seemed to explode in my hand. My hand went numb. I lost my grip.

BOOOM!

He picked it up and fired blindly into the dark. Inches from hitting me.

You know how guns sound on TV? Kind of like

TEWW! TEWW!? Well, in real life, guns don't make cute little popping sounds. They sound like bombs going off.

Ax was still too far off to use his tail. And the Controller was in a panic now. He was firing wildly.

BOOOM! BOOOM! BOOOM!

"Run!" Jake yelled.

So we ran. But the gunfire had attracted other guards. Controllers or just normal human guards, it almost didn't matter. They all had guns.

We hauled, racing through the darkness, feeling betrayed by the noise our own feet made on the concrete walkways.

"This way!" Cassie whispered.

She led us to a door. She yanked on it but it was locked. And we were trapped. There was no turning back.

"Ax," Jake said.

<Yes, Prince Jake.> Ax whipped his tail, faster than the human eye could see.

CHWANG! A neat slice appeared in the steel door, right at the lock mechanism. Cassie tried it again. It opened, and we piled inside. Into a Plexiglas tunnel surrounded by water.

"I always wanted to come see this place," I said. "And look — no crowds."

It was eerie and dark. But not totally dark.

There were red EXIT lights glowing. And moonlight came filtering down through the water in the tanks.

In some ways, that made it a hundred times worse. Without any light, we'd just have been in a dark hallway. But with the light, we could see exactly where we were.

We were in a plastic tunnel beneath millions of gallons of water. Literally, there had to be millions of gallons. Fifty or a hundred swimming pools' worth of water.

And as we trotted down the tunnel, I could see ghostly pale gray shapes gliding by us on both sides and over our heads. Staring fish eyes appeared out of the gloom. Fish mouths gaped silently at us. And long, sleek, cutting shapes seemed to shadow our movements.

<Now, *this* is an interesting human concept,> Ax said approvingly. <This hologram makes it almost appear that we are under the water.>

"Ax? It's not a hologram," Rachel said.

<Then . . . we *are* underwater? Protected only by badly made human plastic?>

"Yeah."

<Why do you humans *do* things like this?>

"Freeze, Andalite!"

It was a new guard. A Controller, too, obviously. He was standing twenty yards up the tunnel. He was in a firing stance, gun leveled at us.

We turned to run back the way we'd come. But the captain came panting around the corner in hot pursuit.

"Trapped!" Cassie said.

"You got 'im, Captain?" the guard called out nervously.

"Yeah!"

"There are some kids with him!"

"Forget the kids. We get kids breaking in here all the time. They're irrelevant. It's the Andalite we want."

<If I go with them peacefully, they may let you all go,> Ax said.

"Forget it," Rachel snapped. "We'll get out of this."

Brave words. But the guards had us trapped. And two very large guns were aimed straight at Ax.

"Jake," I whispered. "This is bad. We need something drastic."

"I'm open to suggestions," he muttered.

"Okay. I suggest you take a deep breath."

"Oh, no. Oh, man."

"Yeah," I agreed. "Everyone take a deep breath. Ax-man? Just how badly made is human plastic?"

It took Ax just a second to figure out what I was talking about.

In a flash, he swung his tail. He swung it in a

big arc. The blade sank into the Plexiglas. And it kept on cutting. It cut a three-foot gash in the plastic, and that was all it took. The water pressure did the rest.

Crrrr-ACCCKK!

FWOOOOOOSSHH!

The water poured in like Niagara Falls.

CHAPTER 15

FWOOOOOSH!

A wave hit me and knocked my legs out from under me. The water picked me up and rocketed me down that Plexiglas tunnel. I went one way, everyone else was blown the other direction.

I saw the captain just ahead of me. I hit him with my feet, doing about fifty miles an hour. He went down and the water rushed over him.

"Jake! Rachel!" I yelled. But no one answered.

Then I couldn't yell anything anymore. The water swept over me, filling the tunnel completely. I fought my way to the top of the tunnel

and tried to suck up a big, squirmy, silver air bubble I saw. I got a mouthful of saltwater instead.

Morph, you idiot! I told myself. I needed to go dolphin. No! Not dolphin. Dolphin needed to be able to reach the surface to breathe. I needed a fish. Long ago we had morphed trout. Could I still retrieve that morph?

All this time I was still shooting along, carried by the rushing water. And then I realized I wasn't alone. There were fish with me. Big fish, little fish. All swimming around me.

Air! I needed air!

Bump! Something hit me. It brushed by me, spinning me around in the water. A body? One of the others? I spun around in the water. And, seeing me move, the shark came back toward me.

I yelped in fear and gave up bubbles of precious air from my lungs. I shot my arms out and kicked my legs hard and backpedaled through the water.

Morph a fish? The shark could eat either one of us!

I began swimming. I had to get back to the break in the tunnel. The hole Ax had made. If I could get through that, I could reach the surface.

Air! Air! My lungs were on fire! I could feel my throat spazzing as my lungs fought to fill themselves.

I swam down that tunnel with the shark following lazily behind.

Is it possible to sweat underwater? I felt like it was. My guts were jelly. My limbs were weak with fear, cramping up from lack of oxygen.

No time to morph. Only time to flee.

There! Was that the hole? Yes! It was a hole. A hole in the tunnel. No, wait. This hole was too round. Too perfectly round.

No time to worry. I kicked hard and started up through the vertical hole. Suddenly my head broke the surface. Air! I sucked it down and spewed it out and sucked it down again, making gasping, sobbing sounds.

Where was I? I was in a sort of vertical tunnel. It was no more than three feet wide. It extended above me for another five or six feet. And at the top there was a metal grill.

"The air-conditioning," I gasped. My voice rang flat and hollow. I was in an air-conditioning vent. This was how they ventilated the tunnel. But I couldn't reach the grill overhead. And I was still treading water.

The shark! I stuck my face back in the water and opened my eyes to look.

I swear I nearly levitated. The shark was rising toward me like some kind of submarine-launched missile. I didn't think, I just reacted. I slammed my feet against one side of the shaft, my hands against the other, and I pressure-walked my way up and out of the water.

My butt was still in the water when I saw that hideous face poke up to take a look at me. That hideous, hammerhead face, with its dead eyes at the end of each side.

That got me up another foot. But the plastic was slippery. And I was too weak to keep it up for long.

"Go kill something else, you monster!" I yelled at the shark.

The head disappeared beneath the water. But I knew in my heart it was still there. Still waiting.

"Ahhh! Ahhh!" My left hand slipped and almost lost it. There was no way this could last. I'd fall. Sooner, not later.

Only one thing to do. I had to acquire that shark.

Animals go limp when you acquire them, I told myself. *Except when they don't. Like Tobias's dolphin.*

This was insane! I couldn't hold on. And if I dropped, my only hope was in actually grabbing hold of a hammerhead shark.

The shark poked his snout above the water again. It was now or never.

"If it turns out you eat me," I told the shark, "make it quick."

I released my pressure. And I dropped. Directly onto the shark.

It turns out, as tough as sharks are, they still aren't used to having screaming, flailing, panic-stricken human beings dropped on them from the sky.

Pah-LOOOSH!

I hit the shark and knocked him downward through the water. The two of us sank together, back into the main tunnel.

Before the shark could recover its wits, I shot out my hand and I grabbed him by the dorsal fin, and I thought, *Please, please, I'm begging you, be like a normal animal and go limp!*

I focused my mind. And to my infinite, profound, world-embracing relief, the hammerhead became peaceful and sluggish.

I wrapped my arms around the big monster, happy I'd worn long sleeves, and we floated up through the gash Ax had made. Up toward air and the stars and freedom.

He was still in an acquisition trance by the time my head broke the surface. We were in one of the tanks. The walls around were higher than

they should have been, since the water had drained out to flood the tunnels. But up around the lip of the tank I saw anxious faces staring down.

"Hey. What are you guys up to?" I asked.

"Marco! You're alive!" Cassie said.

"Yeah. And I brought someone for each of you to meet. Dive on in. It's hammerhead time."

CHAPTER 16

The next day there was a huge headline in the newspaper. A terrible accident at the Ocean World Aquarium. Two guards were missing. Also several fish.

The one guard who did remain told a bizarre tale of a half-deer, half-human creature. The aquarium spokesman sort of implied that the guards must have gotten drunk and shot up the place, causing the tunnel to shatter.

It was on the TV news and everything. CNN even sent a camera crew.

On Monday I handed in five pages of pure, total babble as a book report. I wrote it on the bus. On Thursday I got it back. D-minus. The teacher

wrote, "Nice try, Marco. Do it over, and this time try reading the book."

What can I say? Some teachers buy it. Some don't.

We had decided we couldn't go back to the Royal Island facility until the weekend. Sneaking out at night was risky. If one of us got caught and grounded, we'd be out of business for a while.

I had stopped worrying what the others thought about my running from the sharks. I felt like my actions at the aquarium balanced that out. And I kind of felt like I'd gotten past my fear of sharks. More or less. I mean it's never a good idea to get casual about sharks.

Instead of obsessing over being scared of sharks, I found I was obsessing about the shark DNA inside me. I wanted to morph that shark. I wanted to *be* it. I wanted to know what it felt like to be so relentless, so unafraid. So totally without emotion.

Twice I dreamed about it. Both times in the dream I was a shark, only I still had my own face. And both times someone was doing something terrible. I can't remember what, I just remember thinking, *Oh, man, that's awful.* But in my dream I was a shark, and so whatever the terrible thing was, I was safe.

I wish I could remember what the terrible

thing was. I think maybe it was someone being killed. A woman's voice kept saying, "Help me, help me." I remember that much. But it was confusing because sometimes the voice would start yelling, "Help *him*, help *him*."

After school Thursday, I hung around for a while. I went to the gym. I went to the pool. To my surprise, it was empty. The swim team was somewhere else, I guess. Maybe off shaving their legs and heads. I don't know.

The pool is indoors. It smells of chlorine and mildew. It's one of those places that makes you think about athlete's foot, you know? It's white tile around the sides and dark blue on the bottom. There's a high board and a springboard. There are windows high up on one wall of the room, but mostly the light is fluorescent. There are lights like car high beams in the water itself. But still, it all manages to be gloomy, no matter how many lights are on.

I knew what I was going to do. And I knew it was stupid. But I knew if I didn't do it here, I'd do it in some even stupider place. Like my bathtub at home.

I went to my gym locker and changed into my gym shorts. Then I went back and checked the pool once more. No one. No one in the bleachers. No one in the water. Not a ripple.

I jumped in, feet first, around the eight-foot marker. I bobbed back up to the surface and said, "This is insane, Marco."

To which I answered, "So I'll be careful."

To which I countered, "You're talking to yourself, do you know that?"

"Oh, shut up," I said.

I began to do what I had been wanting to do since Sunday. I began to focus my mind on the shark. I saw it in my memory. Saw it chasing me down that plastic tunnel.

I pictured the moment when I touched the shark's sandpaper skin and brought it under the acquiring spell. And then, slowly, I felt the changes begin.

It started with the squishy sound of my own bones dissolving. See, sharks don't have bones. Just cartilage.

I could hear my bones. The bones in my arms. The bones in my legs. My hip bones, and even my spine, were all starting to dissolve.

I could see down through the water, down to my feet. They shimmered against the deep blue background. They began to elongate. The toes stretched out and out, till each toe was a foot long. My calves followed them, stretching like Gumby. It was a total shock when I realized I was touching the bottom of the pool.

Something was happening to my back. I felt

something growing there, getting larger. It was building itself out of my melting bones.

I reached behind me with my still-human fingers and touched something triangular. I was growing a dorsal fin!

I felt the inside of my mouth itching. Itching amazingly, almost like teething pain.

Shark's teeth were filling my mouth.

Then . . .

"Hey, wuss, get outta the pool!"

There was a loud splash, then another. I spun around. Two heads coming toward me. Two sets of powerful arms churning the water.

Drake and Woo. Two total jerks. Two abject, total bullies. They were also great divers for the school team. At least Drake was. Woo was a complete burnout. He had the I.Q. of cheese.

"Get out of the pool, punk!" Woo said.

"Don't make us kick your butt, Marco-roni," Drake added.

I should have been afraid of them. But I was only afraid they might dive beneath the surface. If they went down there they'd see that I wasn't exactly normal. But from the surface they'd probably just think my ultra-long legs and toes were a distortion.

I started to reverse the morph. I'd been an idiot! I'd left myself open for something like this. Jake would kill me. If he found out. I demorphed as fast as I could. I felt my toes lose contact with the pool bottom.

Then Woo lay back in the water, raised one leg, and kicked me square in the chest with his foot.

I didn't see it coming. Couldn't dodge the blow.

"Ooomph!" The air burst from my lungs. I clutched at my chest.

"Told you to step off," Drake said. "Now we're going to have to stomp you for not having any respect. Unless you want to get your skinny hinder out of the pool."

Drake was giving me a chance to get away. All I had to do was turn around and leave. That was it.

"Yeah, run home to your mommy, Marcoroni," Woo said.

"He can't," Drake said, with a touch of normal humanity in his voice. "His mom's dead."

"Oh, boo hoo," Woo sneered. "Oh, boo hoo, boo hoo." He made a little gesture like he was wiping tears out of his eyes. "His mother probably just ran off with some dude."

All I had to do was walk away. And all I did was to stare at Woo's throat.

I could see the arteries there. The ones that were pulsating on either side of Woo's Adam's apple.

"What are you looking at?" Woo demanded. "You're dead, man, eyeballing me like that."

But I noticed that Woo didn't move toward me. I wanted him to move toward me. I wanted him to.

"What's the matter with his eyes?" Drake asked. "Look at his eyes, man."

"Marco?" It was Jake's voice.

I saw the expression on Woo's face change. He was looking past me now. I heard footsteps on the tile.

"What's up, Marco?" Jake asked, trying to sound casual.

"Ah, isn't that sweet?" Drake said. "Big Jake is here to rescue little Marco-roni."

I swung my heard fiercely toward Jake. I grimaced, baring my teeth. "I thon't neeth you help."

The shark's teeth that filled my mouth distorted my speech. I saw Jake's eyes flare in surprise. Then wary concern.

"Let it go, Marco," Jake said.

I turned back toward Woo. I could still see the pulsing blood just below the skin of Woo's neck. It would be so easy . . .

"He dithed my mom," I said.

"He's not the one responsible for your mother," Jake said. "Don't punish him for the sins of someone else."

I don't know what the two bullies thought of this exchange. I just know they stayed silent. Woo's eyes kept darting from me to Jake. He was confused and worried. Bullies aren't used to hearing their victims talking and acting like they have all the power. Or maybe he didn't like the way I was still staring at his neck.

"Save it for the *real* bad guys, Marco," Jake said.

I let the rest of my shark morph go. I felt the itching in my mouth as my normal teeth replaced the killing shark teeth.

I climbed out of the pool.

"What's the matter with you?" Jake demanded once we were out of there.

I shrugged and forced a smile. "Not a thing, Jake. I guess Woo just looked a little like a fish to me. He look like a fish to you? He does to me."

Not even slightly funny. But it was the best I could do. Jake gave me a long look.

"Maybe you'd better sit out this next mission, Marco."

I laughed. "Jake, you'd have to kill me to keep me away from that island."

CHAPTER 17

Saturday morning, we flew out to the same narrow beach on Royan Island. Now that we knew for sure that the Yeerks were there, just under the water, we were very careful.

But Jake still had time to pull me aside over by a scraggly, twisted tree and ask me if I was all right.

"Sure. Why wouldn't I be all right?"

"Because if you were all right, you'd be busy telling everyone how insane this is and how we're all gonna die. You're weirding everyone out, being so tense."

I just stared at him. "You're telling me it's more relaxing for everyone if I act like we're all going to die?"

97

"It's what they expect from you," Jake said.

"Well, I'll try harder to be entertaining," I said sarcastically.

Jake rolled his eyes. Then he took a quick, cautious glance around. The others were all down on the sand, trying not to notice that Jake and I were having some big heart-to-heart.

Great. Rachel probably thought I was scared and Jake had to give me a pep talk. I still stung from that crack of hers about my being scared of sharks.

"Look, Marco, we're going into a possible battle down there," Jake said, jerking his head toward the water. "Maybe it's time you told the others what's going on with you."

"Nothing is going on with me."

"Marco, your mother is down there."

I flinched. I had been trying really hard not to think about that fact. "How is it going to help the others if I tell them maybe I have my own problems going on here?"

Jake looked surprised. "Marco, I wasn't thinking about it helping the others. I thought it might help you."

I shook my head violently. "No. It doesn't help me to have people pitying me. You know? I went through like a year of pity after my mom died. After she supposedly died. I don't like pity.

Pity makes you feel small and weak. I'd rather have someone hate me than pity me."

Jake sighed. "No one hates you."

"But they would pity me."

Jake didn't have an answer to that.

"Hey, are we doing this?" Rachel called over to us. "Or are you two going to stand there all day yapping?"

"We are doing this," I said forcefully. "But I'll tell you right now, this whole thing is insane. *Insane!* Morphing sharks to infiltrate some underwater Yeerk complex? What has happened to our lives?"

As Jake and I walked back to the others I muttered, "Happy now?"

"Okay," Jake said to everyone. "Ready?"

"I've been ready," Rachel grumbled.

"Everyone remember, this is a new morph," Cassie pointed out. "New instincts to deal with. Be prepared."

See, when you first morph an animal, that animal consciousness can run right over your human mind. It can seize control. And you can't always tell which morphs will be bad. Probably the worst ever were ants.

We waded into the water. All except Tobias, who once again rode on Rachel's shoulder. Four humans, a bird, and an Andalite.

99

"We're a scruffy, weird-looking bunch, aren't we?" I said.

"And short," Rachel said with a sweetly poisoned smile. "Or at least some of us are."

"We'll all have the same-sized dorsal fin in a few minutes, Mighty Xena," I said to her.

Rachel laughed. She pretends to hate it when I call her Xena: Warrior Princess. But I know she's flattered by it.

"Hey, Tobias," I said. "You realize there are no mice underwater, right?"

See, I was doing my job. Playing my part within the group. Teasing. Joking. Exaggerating. That was my role. Like Jake had pointed out: A Marco not making jokes just worries people.

I waded into the surf. It was rougher than it had been the week before. Two and three foot waves were crashing and boiling around me. The sky was darker, grayer.

I tried to put all my problems out of my mind. I tried to wash away the image of my mother. I remembered her two different ways. As the mom I'd always known. And now, as Visser One, the Controller who had arranged to let us escape from captivity in the Yeerk Pool ship, just to embarrass her nemesis, Visser Three.

I tried to shove both images aside. But as I felt the morph begin, I thought, *I'm coming to save you, Mom.* And I also thought, *I'm coming to destroy you, Visser One.*

The morph began differently than it had during my partial morph in the pool. This time it was my skin that changed first.

Dolphins have skin like gray rubber or latex. Sharks have skin like fine-grained sandpaper. Shark skin can leave human skin bloody just by rubbing against it. It's actually made up of millions of *denticles.* Those are tiny, mutated teeth. Sharks are coated with tiny teeth.

As I watched, my tanned arms turned gray. My legs turned gray. My chest and shoulders, all gray.

My feet were twisting together weirdly, as if they were a pair of straws I was braiding. When a wave rolled into me, I lost balance and went backward into the water.

My hand scraped along the bottom. When I looked at it, I realized I'd cut myself on a shell. A few drops of my own blood dribbled into the saltwater.

But I had other things to worry about. Besides, when I demorphed, the cut would be gone.

When I tried to stand back up, I realized my legs were gone. I had a tail now, made of gracefully swooping triangles.

Everything on a shark is triangles. Two elon-

101

gated, joined triangles make the tail. Triangles form the dorsal fins. And hard white serrated triangles fill the mouth with the weapons of destruction.

I used my arms to windmill the water and keep my head up. In flashes between waves I saw the others. A hideous Rachel, with a shark mouth and blond hair; an awesome Ax, with Andalite stalk eyes rising from the bulging hammer's head; Tobias, with feathers melting into gray sandpaper. Not even Cassie could make this morph pretty.

I felt the teeth growing, replacing my own pathetic human teeth. And at the same time, my eyes were moving. They were rotating out to the sides of my head. I lost the ability to focus and kept trying to aim my eyes, to see in three dimensions like I can normally. But my eyes were moving too fast, too far. All I could see was a blur of water and eerie faces.

The hammerhead didn't grow out of the side of my head. It grew out of the front. Like pillars of flesh were growing beneath my eyeballs, then taking those eyes out to the side.

My arms shriveled and became sharp fins. I was entirely underwater now. Just in time, my lungs collapsed into nothing and slits like open wounds formed where my neck had been.

I had gills. And shark's teeth. And I had shark's eyes.

But I still had not felt the shark's mind. Not until I was completely in the water and began to move. Only then did I feel the shark's mind, its instincts, come bubbling up through my own human awareness.

It was the movement that set it off. See, sharks cannot be still. If a shark stops moving, he dies. A shark is movement. Restless, relentless, eternal movement.

I felt my fear leave me.

I felt my anger leave as well.

My every emotion and feeling simply lifted away. And I was glad. Because now I was clear. Now I saw the world with perfect simplicity. Perfect understanding.

The world, you see, is nothing but prey. And I was nothing but hunger. There was nothing else. No mother or father, no fear or joy, no worry.

Hunger. Prey. Hunger. Prey.

I turned away from the shore and swam out to sea. And then, I stopped. The last vestiges of my human mind were swept aside.

The shark sensed blood.

CHAPTER 18

Sharks had been swimming Earth's oceans for hundreds of millions of years already when the ancestors of Homo sapiens were still trying to figure out how to peel a banana.

People will tell you, "Oh, you don't need to be afraid of sharks. They have more reason to fear humans than humans have to fear sharks."

True. Humans kill far more sharks than sharks kill humans. Will that fact make you feel any better if a shark chomps you in two at the waist? Probably not.

Sharks are killing machines. Mostly they kill fish. In some parts of the world they kill seals. They kill dolphins. They kill whales, when they can manage it. And they kill humans. At least some species do: the great white, the tiger shark . . . and the hammerhead.

This was the killing machine I had become. Utterly without fear. Utterly without emotion. A mind with no room for anything else but killing. There was nothing playful, like you'd find with a lion. Nothing in the shark that cared about family or children. No sense of belonging. Just a solitary creature of sharp, cutting triangles. A restless, ever-moving thing, ever questing after blood.

A mind as cold, as sharp, as deadly as a polished-steel knife blade. That was the mind that gathered my confused human consciousness up and swept it along in the endless search for something to kill and eat.

The shark turned toward the scent of blood. My long tail pushed lazily at the water. My hammerhead worked like a diving plane to let me turn this way and that. My vision was surprisingly good. Almost as good as human vision.

I could hear. And I could feel other senses that were unlike anything human. When fish passed close by, I felt a tingling from their electrical current. And at some deep, hard-to-grasp level, I realized I could sense the very magnetic field of planet Earth. I knew north and south without knowing the words.

But mostly, I could smell. I could smell the water as I sucked it in, relentlessly sampling. And right now, I could smell blood.

I was aware of the others nearby. I knew they were sharks like me. But I didn't care. I was on the trail of blood.

I followed the scent of the blood. No more than a few drops of blood, a thin, wispy trail diluted in billions of gallons of surging seawater, but I smelled it.

I followed the scent through the water. If the scent was stronger in my left nostril, I veered left. If it was stronger on my right, I veered right. It would lead me to prey. It would lead me to food. The blood trail had come from very close by! I could sense it, and a cold excitement seized me.

Blood! A wounded animal! Prey!

But as I turned and turned again, circling back toward more shallow water, I became frustrated. Where was it? Where was the bleeding creature? Where was my prey?

The others circled nearby. One of them brushed against me, sandpaper on sandpaper. They were seeking it, too. The bleeding prey whose scent filled our heads.

Where was it?

The shark brain was confused, uncertain. And in that moment of confusion and uncertainty, the steel mind of the shark left a slight crack. Enough of a crack. Enough for my human brain to call up the picture of a human hand, bleeding from a small cut.

My hand! *My* hand. The human named Marco.

<Oh, my God!> I yelled in thought-speak. <It was me! It's my blood! That's my own blood!>

The others didn't care. They continued to turn in ever tighter circles, looking, searching, marauding for the source of the blood.

<Jake! Jake! Shake it off, man. The shark has you. Jake, come on, man. Get on top of it. Cassie! Rachel. Ax. Tobias. All of you. It's the shark instincts. Fight them. That was my blood.>

It took a few minutes before we were all back to being ourselves. Tobias dealt with it easiest. I guess that's not a surprise. He's a predator normally. Maybe the shark mind and the hawk mind aren't so different.

Ax handled it well, too. Not that Andalites are sharklike. It was mostly that he'd morphed a shark already.

<Yikes,> Cassie said, laughing nervously. <Kind of single-minded, aren't they?>

<No one else bleed,> Rachel said. <I'll be hungry for hours.>

We were a little shaken up. We'd gotten cocky

107

about being able to control animal morphs. But the shark was different. I think at some level, at the most basic survival level, that primitive shark brain was actually superior to our own human brain.

It knew what it wanted. And there is a terrible strength in knowing what you want and having no doubts.

We swam around the island, back toward the holographically concealed underwater facility. This time we expected to be able to pass right by the supersharks who had almost taken us out when we'd been in dolphin morph.

We swam right through what looked exactly like seabed, right up to the facility. With dead shark eyes I stared through the portholes. The one that opened onto a busy cubicle area. And the other one. The one that looked into a more private room.

The guard sharks swam right past and around us, never paying the slightest attention.

<That was easy,> Rachel said. <Let's go ahead and do this.>

<Don't forget: The Leerans are psychic at close range,> Ax warned. <Whatever we do, we have to stay clear of them.>

This was the point where I'd normally make a joke. But just then I saw a woman entering the private office. She was distorted by the convex glass, by the water, and by my own water-oriented shark's eyes.

But I knew her.

And I forgot to find something funny to say.

CHAPTER 19

<Now what?> Tobias wondered. <We got past the guard sharks.>

<Now I guess we go take a look inside,> Jake said. He didn't sound too enthusiastic about the idea.

<Two of the three big hatches are open,> Rachel observed. <Eenie, meenie, minie, moe?>

<Heads or tails?> I suggested.

<One potato, two potato?> Cassie said.

<What do these things mean?> Ax asked.

<These are highly advanced human methods for making choices,> I said. <How about the middle door?>

<Middle door,> Jake agreed.

We swam toward the middle door. From a distance it was big. Up close it was even bigger. It was obviously big enough for the submarine to enter through.

From the outside the tunnel inside looked dark, but once away from the filtered green sunlight from above, we could see that there were lights on inside the tunnel.

We swam around, taking our time and trying to look casual. The open door and short tunnel led to a rectangular pool. A boat dock, obviously. Probably used by the submarine. There were other hammerheads there, too. But still they ignored us.

I rose to the surface, letting my dorsal fin slice its way into the air. I rolled to one side, and raised my left eye above the water. Shark eyes are not made for seeing through atmosphere, but I could still see well enough. I saw a wall of corrugated steel that formed the rectangular boat dock we were in. But other than that I could only look straight up at the rafters overhead.

<We're not going to see much more staying in shark morph,> Rachel said. <We need to get out and look around.>

<As what?> Jake asked. <We'd need something that fit in here. Something these Controllers wouldn't notice. But something with decent senses.>

<Flies,> Cassie suggested. <Everyone except Tobias has a fly morph.>

<Oh, great. I get left out again,> Tobias complained.

<I think the bad guys might notice a red-tailed hawk flying around in their underwater facility,> I said. <Although there are probably rats infesting this place, too, so the Controllers may appreciate your being here to eat their pests.>

<We'd have to morph back to human underwater,> Jake pointed out. <Then morph to fly. All without drowning.>

Scr-EET! Scr-EET! Scr-EET!

<What's that?>

<An alarm! Oh, man. They know we're here!>

Suddenly a rush of hammerheads was coming straight for us. I saw them first as dark shadows in the water. They loomed larger and larger. We turned to face them. But it was impossible. There had to be fifty of them!

On they came, whipping the water with their long tails.

Then . . . they swam past. They kept swimming for the far end of the dock. And now we could distinctly hear the sound of a mechanized door opening.

WHRRREEEEEEEE!

<Those are definitely *not* normal sharks,> Cassie said.

<Let's follow them,> Rachel said. <They may lead us where we need to go.>

<Yeah, or they might lead us right into where they make the new Oscar Mayer Shark-meat Lunchables,> I said. <Hammerhead slices, American cheese, crackers, and a cookie.>

We went after the sharks. We followed them to the far end of the dock. A new door had opened. There was actually a line of sharks waiting to get in. The pathway narrowed till soon we were single file.

<I'm starting to think Marco was right,> Tobias said. <This sure feels like some kind of shark slaughterhouse.>

<I don't think so,> Cassie said. <I'll bet this is something more medical. Besides, we'd smell blood if the other sharks were getting hurt.>

<Unless they're getting boiled alive,> I said. <Boiled and canned, and in one process. Then it's Chicken of the Sea shark meat.>

Suddenly I heard Cassie yell, <Ahhh!>

She was right in front of me. And before I could react, I knew why she had yelled. Steel claws reached out from each side and grabbed me just behind my hammer head. The claws held me tightly, but not painfully. I was drawn upward till I was vertical. I was out of the water. My gills gasped in the air. My body writhed in panic.

I saw a line of us. A conveyor belt of hammerhead sharks, all hanging vertically. There were human-Controllers and Hork-Bajir manning equipment boards and looking totally uninterested.

We turned a corner into a second room and up rose a robot arm festooned with tools whose purpose I couldn't even guess. The robot arm arced toward the shark two spaces ahead of Cassie. From out of nowhere a long, thick needle appeared. It plunged into the back of the shark's head.

<What the . . . We have to get outta here!> I cried.

But there was no time. The conveyor belt kept moving. Too fast!

The robot arm moved with machine precision. It plunged the needle into the back of Cassie's head.

<It's okay,> Cassie managed to gasp. <I think it was just an immunization. Maybe.>

But what came next was not okay. The robot arm hesitated. It popped out a sort of metal detector or something and moved it over Cassie's shark head. Then it extruded a drill.

Not like a dental drill. Like a drill you'd use to make holes in wood.

The drill bit spun and it plunged.

<What was that?!> Cassie cried in alarm.

The drill bit withdrew. But a bright steel probe lanced into the hole. In it poked, then withdrew. A wisp of smoke curled away from the hole as it was cauterized by a green laser beam.

<Cassie! Are you okay?> Jake yelled.

<Uh . . . yeah. I guess so.>

And then it was my turn. There was a sharp prick of pain, but sharks don't care about pain.

The drill withdrew. And seconds later, I was dropped into saltwater. In fact, I quickly realized, I was back in the same boat dock I'd been in before. There were other hammerheads all around me. My friends were being dropped practically on top of me.

<What was *that* all about?> Tobias asked.

<They injected us all with something,> Cassie said. <Right into our brains. But . . . oh. Oh! Aaaarrggghhh!>

It hit me a few seconds later. How can I describe the pain? You know how I said sharks don't care about pain? Well, this wasn't any pain that any shark had endured. I felt my brain exploding. Like some mad animal was trapped inside my head and trying to claw its way out.

I screamed. <Aaaahhhhh! Oh, oh, oh! Stop it!>

And then, through the water, a sound reverberated. Like a WHOOO-WHOOO-WHOOO.

The pain stopped. In its place came a wave of pleasure. It was like the taste of prey in my shark mouth: the ultimate shark pleasure.

<What is happening?> Ax demanded.

<I don't know, but it's kind of nice.>

Then, the weirdest thing . . . I felt the shark mind, that simple killing-machine mind, seem to open up. The shark mind looked out through its eyes, and for the first time ever, noticed things that had nothing to do with finding prey.

The shark eyes noticed the pattern of the corrugated steel that formed the dock. The shark sense of smell took note of scents like oil and rust and seaweed that had nothing to do with killing and eating.

<This sounds insane,> I said, <but I think this shark is getting smarter.>

<Like the sharks that attacked us,> Rachel agreed.

<My shark brain just wondered,> Cassie said, sounding amazed. <It wondered whether there would be prey later.>

<That sounds sharklike,> Jake said.

<No!> Cassie yelled excitedly. <Sharks don't "wonder." Sharks can't even form the concept of a future, let alone wonder about it. It's completely impossible!>

<So what does it mean?> Tobias asked.

Cassie answered. <It's the Yeerks. They've altered these brains. That's why the sharks were able to work together the other time. The Yeerks

are mutating these shark brains. We just got the first treatment.>

<Why?> Rachel wondered.

Ax said, <There's only one reason to alter the physiology of these brains. To make it possible for the Yeerks to enter them. The natural shark brain is too small, too simplistic for the Yeerks to control. They are mutating the sharks to make them capable of being made into Controllers. They will need to add ear canals as well. So that the Yeerks can enter and leave the brain.>

<A new version of Hork-Bajir,> I said. <That's it! The Yeerks want water-going Hork-Bajir. They need dangerous, tough, deadly shock-troops that can go where Hork-Bajir can't: in the water. What better soldier than a *shark*-Controller, if you need troops in an underwater environment?>

<Yes,> Tobias agreed grimly. <And what worse nightmare for any peaceful species to face?>

CHAPTER 2D

<We have to find out more,> Jake said. <It's time to get out of the water and go look around in this place.>

It was going to be hard and dangerous. We had to return to human form. Then morph again. All in the water. Without being seen, or drowning.

I was relieved to be getting out of the shark morph. I hated sharks, I'd decided. I didn't want to be one anymore. Let alone a sort of super, self-aware, thinking shark.

I was happy when my legs reappeared. When my fins became hands, when my teeth ground and itched away and became the tiny, blunt, piti-fully weak human teeth.

But I knew I'd never hold my breath clear into

a new morph. I poked my head above the surface and looked around with human eyes for the first time. The others popped up nearby. Tobias looked like a drowned rat. He stood on Rachel's head.

There was a dark ceiling high overhead. And I could hear machinery. But I saw no humans or Hork-Bajir or Taxxons standing around the dock. Maybe they were all busy back in that office room we'd seen through the portholes.

"Looks kind of empty," I whispered to Jake.

"Yeah. We'd better be careful, though. Morph here in the water. It won't be any problem for the fly, I don't think."

He was right. The water didn't bother the fly morph. Something else did.

I focused on the fly DNA within me, and I began to shrink. I had done the fly morph several times before, so I was prepared for the way the spiky legs grew out of my chest. The way all my internal organs melted away, replaced by simpler insect organs. The way my mouth and nose sprouted out to become a horrible, long *proboscis*.

I was in the water, breathing air from a bubble, when it began. I realized my head was exploding. And that was not just an expression.

<Aaaahhh! Aaaahhh!> I screamed. My head was still maybe two inches wide, almost entirely

fly, with only a few shreds of human left. But I stopped the morph instantly.

I stared around me with eyes more fly than human. The watery world was a shattered mirror of images. The fly's compound eyes saw with a thousand tiny, irregular, bewildering TV sets, each tuned to a slightly different channel. And because we were underwater, I saw even less than usual.

But then, by luck, Rachel drifted near. Just within range.

Seeing a morph is always horrifying. I mean, we get used to it, but it never stops being creepy beyond belief. And nothing is creepier than watching a human being turn into a fly. Trust me, that is enough fuel to keep you in nightmares the rest of your life.

But what I had just seen, floating past me in the water, was worse.

<Everyone, stop morphing! Stop now!> I yelled, just as the others all started groaning in agony.

<What is it?> Ax asked. <I am experiencing a terrible pain.>

<I'm not surprised. Demorph! They put something in us.>

<What are you talking about?> Rachel asked.

<I mean when the Yeerks drilled into us, they

left something inside! When we shrank to fly size, this thing, this whatever it is, was too big! Our fly bodies were smaller than the thing inside us. We'd have killed ourselves.>

<What did it look like?> Tobias asked.

I surfaced again, human once more. "I couldn't tell. I just saw Rachel's head being all twisted and bulging from trying to shrink with this thing inside it!"

"Some kind of control device," Jake said. "I should have realized! That's why we got drilled when the other sharks didn't. We didn't have the control device in our heads. The Yeerks are using it to control the sharks until all the treatments are done."

<That's what caused that surge of pleasure,> Tobias said. <The Yeerks use that feeling to keep the sharks happy. To summon them and control them. Make them forget the pain of the brain mutation. It's tied to the underwater sounds they broadcast.>

"So what do we do?" I asked.

"We get these things out of our heads!" Rachel yelled. "If we have to stomp every Yeerk in this facility!"

"Oh, good, the subtle approach," I sneered.

"Rachel may be right," Jake said. "We can't have this. Period. We cannot have Yeerk control

devices in our heads. We're underwater, with implants in our brains, and psychic Leeran aliens running around. This is seriously not cool."

"There may be hundreds of Controllers here," I pointed out. "We can't just get crazy and get away with it."

"No," Jake agreed. "But we need a distraction. Two teams: one to get to the controls of this place. The other to, as Marco said, get crazy and keep the Yeerks busy. Ax, Marco, and Tobias in the first group. Rachel, Cassie, and me to cause a distraction."

"Finally. We get to *do* something."

That was Rachel, of course.

CHAPTER 21

⊓e, Ax, and Tobias. We couldn't morph anything small with the Yeerk control devices still implanted in our heads. Not bugs, anyway. So how we were supposed to go wandering around the underwater facility without being noticed?

"I think someone might notice a pair of wolves running around," I said. "We need to go airborne. The bird heads are obviously big enough to allow for the control chips. After all, Tobias returned to his normal hawk body okay. Besides, people have a tendency not to look up."

A few minutes later, I was in osprey morph. Ax was a northern harrier. Tobias was Tobias. And we were all wet.

A wet bird is not a happy bird, I can tell you that.

We flapped, unseen, up to the roof of the facility. It was made with open steel beams. You know: like the inside of a Toys "R" Us store. There was a slight curvature to the roof, probably to help carry the load of water pressure.

From up near the ceiling we could perch and look down at the entire facility. There were three identical dock slips like the one we'd been in. One housed the transparent sub. There was no one aboard but a couple of Taxxons doing maintenance work.

We saw two buildings separated from each other by the center dock. The buildings were identical, windowless rectangles painted white. Like warehouses. There were other smaller buildings around as well. The kinds of buildings they use as "temporary" classrooms.

<Big mistake,> Tobias pointed out. <No windows. I guess it never occurred to them they might want to be able to see around inside this place. The only windows look out into the water.>

<They aren't expecting enemies in here. No one is supposed to make it past the sharks,> Ax said.

<Whatever is happening is happening inside those buildings,> Tobias said. <So which one do we go for? Left or right?>

<The one on the right,> I said instantly.

<Why?>

I couldn't tell him that was the building that connected to the big porthole with the grand but empty office behind it. The office I was sure was my mother's. <Because Jake will attack the other one,> I said, <and we can't be wherever he and the others are causing trouble.>

<Fine. Next question: How do we get inside?>

<With incredible timing, that's how,> I said. As we watched, a Taxxon came writhing and shimmying out through the one door. Its sides scraped as it pushed through.

<Next Taxxon to come out, we go in,> I said.

<What if another Taxxon doesn't come out?> Ax wondered.

<Don't you Andalites believe in luck?>

<No.>

<Me neither. How about hope?>

<We believe in hope.>

<Good. Now me, I believe in Jake. See him over behind the left building? The tiger? I think he's just about ready to —>

"Grrrrooooaaaaarrrrr!"

<— do that.>

The roar was the roar of a tiger. A noise that could make adults want to crawl in bed with their teddy bears and pull the blankets over their heads.

The effect on the Taxxon in the doorway was instantaneous. He decided to back up.

<Oh, man! Okay, we go now!> I said. I released my talon grip on the steel cross-beam, swept my wings back to gain speed, aimed for that doorway, opened my wings, adjusted my tail, and blew just over the Taxxon's heaving, squirming back at about fifty miles an hour.

<Yah-HAH! Oh, man, that's still fun!>

A harrier and a red-tailed hawk were milliseconds behind me.

Past the distracted Taxxon without being seen! Through the doorway, way too fast! A long hallway. The *end* of the long hallway, coming up way, way, WAY too fast!

<Look out!>

<Turn!> Tobias yelled.

<Where?>

<Doorway! *Now!*> Tobias practically screamed.

I banked my wings and shot through an open side door, scraping my back and my right wing on the doorjamb.

A room. A desk. A chair. Walls! Walls! Walls!

I flared to kill my speed, but not enough.

<Left!> Tobias yelled.

I banked an amazingly sharp left and flew through a second doorway into an almost totally dark room. I was no longer going fifty miles an hour. I was probably only doing about fifteen. But let me tell you: Flying at fifteen miles an hour in a dark room where you can't see the walls is slightly too exciting.

<Tight circle!> Tobias said. <Tighter, spiral down, get ready to land!>

WHUMPF!

WHUMPF!

CRASH! Rattle . . . rattle . . .

Ax had hit the desk. Tobias had hit the floor. I had hit a metal trash can and gone rolling inside it.

<Everyone okay?> I asked.

<I have damaged my bird body,> Ax said calmly, <but I am alive.>

<Me, too,> I said, testing a painful tail. <I think I broke my tail.>

<Good grief. This is the last time I ever fly through a building with you two amateurs,> Tobias said.

<Okay, let's demorph,> I said. <There's no one around, and Ax and I aren't going to be flying till we *re*morph.>

With my excellent osprey hearing, I could make out sounds of damage and destruction coming from somewhere outside.

<What do you think Rachel morphed?> Tobias asked. <Elephant or bear?>

<She'd do them both at the same time if she could figure out how,> I muttered.

I demorphed as quickly as I could. We'd done a lot of morphing in a very short period of time. I was getting tired. But still, within a few minutes, it was me as human, Tobias morphed into his human shape, and Ax as his own Andalite self.

"You know, sometimes there's just a very fine line between us and the Three Stooges," I said.

<What are stooges?> Ax asked.

"A stooge is a guy stupid enough to run around inside a Yeerk stronghold wearing a pair of bike shorts and accompanied by a Deer-man from outer space and a mouse-eating Bird-boy. That's a stooge."

I led the way from the darkened room. Ax came behind, tail at the ready. Tobias walked awkwardly at the rear. He's still getting used to being able to be human again.

"I can't believe I lived most of my life with these lame human eyes," he grumbled. "You people are blind."

"Shhh."

I crept out into a brightly lit hallway. I took a second to try and figure out which direction to go. At the end of the hallway was a door, different from the others. On it was a gold symbol of some kind. Like the presidential seal.

"That way. Ax? If anyone pops out of any of these doors . . ." I let it hang. Ax knew what to do. He twirled the bladed end of his tail, limbering it up, I guess.

We scurried down the hallway. I reached for the door handle. I opened it.

"Come in," a voice said.

I froze there. My head poking through the open door. My friends were hidden behind me.

"I said come in," a sinister voice said. "Never make me give an order twice. You won't live to hear me give it a third time."

So I stepped through the doorway, closing it quickly behind me, blocking Ax and Tobias from view.

And I walked on wooden, rickety legs to the big desk in the center of the room. I walked over and stood there. Facing her. Facing my mother.

CHAPTER 22

She looked the same.

But she also looked different.

Same dark eyes, same mouth, same movie-star hair. But there was a different soul looking out through those eyes. They were hard eyes. Mean eyes. Ruthless, pitiless eyes.

Like the eyes of a shark. No more gentle or sweet than the cold, eerie eyes of a hammerhead shark.

I was glad. You see, I had wondered whether she had been a Controller for long before she faked her own death. I had wondered whether it was a Yeerk kissing me good night, and teasing me about my vanity, and laughing at my dumb jokes.

But now I felt like I knew. It couldn't have been, see, because she did look different. I could see the evil inside her. I would have seen it back then. Right?

Part of my brain said, *Don't be a fool, Marco. She's among her fellow Yeerks now. Of course she's no longer putting on an act. She doesn't have to hide what she is anymore.*

My mother looked at me with the eyes of a Yeerk visser. "I was expecting four new technicians. Where are the other three?"

I just stared.

"Where are the other three who were supposed to come with you from the Pool ship?"

I jerked my head to break the spell. "The other three? The other three technicians? Oh. Um . . . they, uh, they had a problem. I think Visser Three killed them for doing something wrong."

It was possibly the stupidest lie I have ever told. And yet it worked.

My mother raised one eyebrow contemptuously. "If that clown Visser Three thinks he can damage me in the eyes of the Council of Thirteen by sabotaging this project, he's a bigger fool than I thought."

I gulped. From outside there came a huge roar and a beastly bellow. Jake and Rachel and Cassie. Still creating a distraction. I could only imagine how desperate their situation was.

"We're having a bit of a problem with the Andalite bandits Visser Three has still failed to exterminate," Visser One said calmly.

All I could do was nod.

"I see," she said. "Obviously your host mind is giving you some trouble. I'm sure you are aware that your host body is the biological son of my own host body."

Not a shred of emotion. Not a shred of guilt. It was sitting there, using my mother's body, knowing . . . knowing, like no one else could possibly know, the agony my mother must be feeling at seeing me.

I nodded. "Yes, Visser."

"You must learn to control your host more completely. My own host is in here creating an awful racket," she said, tapping her head. "But I do not let her weeping and wailing disturb me."

"No, Visser," I said in a whisper. "I will try harder to control my host."

I wanted to destroy that Yeerk. I wanted to reach inside that familiar head and rip that filthy Yeerk out of there and stomp it into the floor.

I was surprised Visser One couldn't see my hate. I felt it vibrating the very air around me.

But I couldn't do anything. All I could do was stand there. Stand there with my arms at my sides and listen to the foul Yeerk visser, highest of all the vissers, sneer at the fact that my mother's mind and heart were crying from seeing her son made a slave of the Yeerks.

WHAM!

It was the sound of something large being slammed against the outside wall of the building. I pictured a Hork-Bajir thrown by a rampaging elephant.

Visser One barely blinked. "Well. I guess I'd better see to this little problem outside," she said wearily. "I have to wrap up this shark project and have a thousand shark-Controllers ready for use on Leeran within two months. I don't need to be pestered by Visser Three's leftover Andalite problems. That incompetent fool will be arriving soon. I only wish these tiresome Andalite bandits would remove that particular annoyance from my life."

She stood up. She straightened her hair exactly the way my mom always did. I looked into her eyes, wishing I could see some sign there of my mother. Wishing I could tell her, "Don't worry, Mom, I'm not a Controller. I'm fighting, Mom. I'm fighting them and some day I'll save you."

But that would have been fatal. And I'm not someone who does emotional, stupid things. Sometimes I wish I were.

"Get to the lab," Visser One said. "Go to work."

She walked past me, like she'd already forgotten I existed. I held my breath as she stepped out into the hallway. But Ax and Tobias were gone.

I breathed a sigh of relief. Why? Maybe because Ax would have hurt her. I don't know.

Then, through the massive round porthole, I saw something large and sinuous. Like a snake. But a snake that was fifty feet long and thicker than a Taxxon.

It was the yellow of poison. With a mouth that looked able to swallow a small boat.

It was coming straight for the facility. And on either side of it, like an honor guard, were a dozen Hork-Bajir in bizarre red diving suits, propelled by small water jets attached to each ankle.

I had a feeling I knew this particular snake's name.

CHAPTER 23

I followed her out in the hall, but she walked away. Swaggering. Like the Yeerk visser she was.

I watched her for longer than I should have. Then I ducked into a side door. The room was dark. I expected to find Ax and Tobias there. I did. I found Ax very suddenly, in fact.

THWAPP!

A tail blade was pressed against my throat.

"Hey, it's me. Please don't remove my head. I use it sometimes."

<Marco!>

"We were just trying to figure out whether we should try and rescue you or go join the fight outside," Tobias said in his now-unfamiliar human voice.

<We accessed the central computer for this facility. But before we could discover anything, you came in.>

Ax led me over to a glowing, three-dimensional computer display. It was weird, the way most of the place was like any standard, boring human office. Like an insurance agent's or a school secretary's office. But I guess the Yeerks didn't want to be stuck messing with human-level computers.

"Roooaaaarrrr!"

Jake's tiger roar sounded a little frazzled.

"We need to get out there and help them," Tobias said.

"No," I snapped. "They can't be helped by us rushing out there. Visser Three is coming with more Hork-Bajir. He's morphed this giant snake from planet Whatever."

They stared at me like I must be hallucinating or something.

"Look, it's him, okay? I saw it through the porthole. A huge yellow sea snake with Hork-Bajir alongside. Who do you figure that would be?"

<He cannot have had time to hear about a battle down here,> Ax pointed out. <It's too quick to be a rescue mission.>

"I don't think it is a rescue mission. I think

it's a coincidence. I think he happened to be on his way here."

"Just our bad luck," Tobias said.

"Maybe not," I pointed out. "Visser One and Three are rivals. Visser One let us escape to mess with Visser Three. This may work for us. But first things first. Ax? Start questioning that computer."

I couldn't believe I was standing there so calmly while Jake, Rachel, and Cassie were probably fighting for their lives. But I guess I'd had a good look at the ruthlessness of the Yeerks. I'd seen it in Visser One's cold eyes. I'd heard it in the pitiless voice that didn't care one tiny bit that I was the son of the body it now controlled.

I guess there are times when the only way to survive is to be as ruthless as the enemy. To destroy before you can be destroyed.

<As we guessed,> Ax said, staring with his main eyes at the computer readout. <The Yeerks are invading Leeran. It isn't going well for them. Most of the Leerans are resisting. Since the Leerans are psychic, it's impossible for the Yeerks to deceive them. So the Yeerks have decided to forget about stealth and go to a straight invasion by force.>

"But it's a watery world, so they can't rely on Hork-Bajir," I said. "It's true. The hammerheads

137

are being reengineered to allow for Yeerks to make them Controllers. The shark-Controllers will be the troops in the war for Leeran."

"Great. Now can we get out there and help Rachel and the others?" Tobias demanded.

He hadn't waited for an answer. He was already demorphing. Red-tailed feathers were sprouting from his hands.

"Ax, can you find a way to remove these things in our heads?" I asked.

Ax communicated mentally with the computer. <There is a liquidation program but it's heavily encrypted. The only other way the implants can be liquidated is in the event this facility is completely destroyed.>

"What?" Tobias said. "You can't eliminate these things without blowing up the whole place?"

<Yes. It's so there would be no evidence left behind if something goes wrong. But in any case, we don't have a way to annihilate this facility.>

"Ax. How do they keep the water out of this place? How do they keep it from flooding? If it were just air pressure our ears would be seriously imploding."

<Force fields, I assume. Modulated to hold the water back while allowing animal life-forms to enter and leave.>

"Can you reach the controls?"

<Done.>

"Can you turn off the force fields? Without letting the Yeerks know?"

Ax laughed derisively. <I'm an Andalite. No simple, derivative, unimaginative Yeerk computer presents any difficulties to me, you know, unless it's specially shielded.>

<What are you doing?> Tobias demanded, once more back in hawk morph. <You let the water in and we'll *all* be killed.>

"Destroy the facility and it may trigger the liquidation of these head implants," I said. "Ax, can you build in a five-minute delay?"

<Five minutes?> He communicated with the computer by thought-speak. <Done. In five minutes, millions of your gallons of water will come rushing into this place.>

<We'd better all have gills before then,> Tobias said.

"Yeah. And those who can't grow gills . . . I guess they'll wish they could."

CHAPTER 24

We ran from the room. I morphed as I ran. I morphed into a gorilla. We were going into a fight. And although the gorilla isn't a mean or aggressive animal, it is amazingly powerful.

By the time we reached the door to the outside, I was done. Tobias was already flying, and Ax was Ax.

I threw open the door to the outside. Actually, I forgot I was in gorilla morph and opened the door so hard it ripped clear off its hinges.

What I saw was a scene of destruction. There were injured Hork-Bajir lying crumpled around the facility. There was a reeking, squashed Taxxon being munched on ravenously by a fellow Taxxon. Rachel in grizzly morph, Jake in tiger morph, and Cassie as a wolf had done some serious damage. But now they were cornered, almost surrounded by wary but determined Hork-Bajir.

Visser One, my mother, was striding toward them, seemingly unconcerned. As she went, she was kicking the wounded Hork-Bajir, demanding they get up and fight. Half a dozen had already rallied to her.

<Five minutes,> I said tersely. <Less. Then, we have to be in the water.>

<With gills,> Tobias reminded me.

<Okay, let's go save Jake,> I said. <That guy. He's always needing me to come along and rescue his butt.>

I broke into a loping run. Tobias flapped away. And Ax ran, tail at the ready.

<At least I can introduce Visser One to my tail!> Ax said gleefully.

<No!> I yelled. <I mean, you guys go help the others. I'll clean up Visser One and her group.>

Ax and Tobias went ahead. I hit the group of Hork-Bajir that was following my mother. They didn't see me coming.

WHAM! I slammed a Hork-Bajir down to the concrete and he stayed down.

SWISH! A Hork-Bajir spun around and swung his arm, wrist blade turning toward me. But he'd already been wounded. He was slow. I was slow, too. But I didn't miss. I drove my canned-ham-sized gorilla fist, with more power than ten Evander Holyfields, into the Hork-Bajir's chest. The other Hork-Bajir stayed back.

My mother turned around. "Kill it, you cowards! Kill it!"

One of the Hork-Bajir leaped at me, arms and legs all flashing with deadly blades. I tried to dodge, but gorillas are not exactly fast.

<Aaaahhhh!> I was cut! My left arm was slashed deeply. Blood was flowing out onto my dark, coarse fur.

"That's it! Kill it!" Visser One crowed gleefully.

The Hork-Bajir cut me again, less deeply but more painfully, with a blow that sliced through my rubbery gorilla muzzle. His buddies decided it was safe to come after me now, too.

They were wrong. I was a gorilla. People might look at a gorilla and think, *Well, it's only twice as heavy as a big man, and not even as tall. So how strong could it be?*

How strong? You could hit a gorilla in the head with a sledgehammer and he'd just grab it and make you eat it. Arnold Schwarzenegger using his entire body could not have bent back my wrist if I didn't want him to. In the wild, gorillas are gentle, sweet animals. But I wasn't just a gorilla. I was Marco with the power of a gorilla. And the Marco part of me was not feeling gentle or sweet.

I grabbed the big Hork-Bajir by his snake neck. Grabbed him with one hand and closed my fingers tight. He slashed at me wildly. He cut my arm again and again. But I held on. And with my other arm I grabbed another Hork-Bajir by the wrist. Then I simply introduced them to each other. The hard way.

They decided that was enough. They left. And Visser One stood alone.

Just me and Visser One. Just me and my mother.

"So, Andalite," she said calmly. "I see you are enjoying the use of all these wonderful Earth morphs. But you must know you cannot escape from this place. However, if you surrender peacefully, I can let you live."

I didn't say anything. I couldn't. The Yeerks think we're all Andalites. That's what we want them to go on thinking. We've always worried that if we started talking to them we might let something slip that would tell them we're human.

If they ever find out what we really are, we're done for.

But there was a second reason I couldn't talk to Visser One. See, I knew if I started talking to

my mom, I would never be able to stop myself. I'd spill it all out. I'd tell her everything because it's been so long since I've been able to talk to her. I've thought about it many times. Many, many times. All the things I'd like to tell her. About my life. My friends. What I did in school. How I made some teacher laugh.

Visser One's so-familiar eyes flickered. "If you kill me, you'll die as well, Andalite."

And then I heard a rasping, rumbling, almost belching voice. It said, *"Ha tu ma el ga su fa to li."* An alien voice speaking an alien language. But I understood it. I felt it in my mind. It was like thought-speak, only this was deeper, more profound. This voice seemed to use my own words in my own brain.

What it said was, *Don't be fooled, Visser One, this is no Andalite.*

I spun around. And there, standing just behind me, was a Leeran-Controller, its tentacles waving. I could squash the big amphibian without breaking a sweat. But I just froze. I froze and looked back at my mother.

It is not Andalite, the Leeran said again. *It is a human.*

Visser One's face remained impassive. "No, you idiot," she sneered. "It's a gorilla. They are related to humans, but not human. This is an Andalite in morph."

I beg your pardon for disagreeing, Visser, but —

Two things happened then, within seconds of each other.

I broke out of my trance, whipped around and punched the Leeran right in his froggy mouth.

And from the nearby dock a huge yellow serpent reared up suddenly.

"Visser Three, I assume," my mother said contemptuously.

<Well, I see you've made a mess of things, Visser One. Our old friends the Andalite bandits seem to be annihilating most of your troops.>

"I'd have more troops, but for your interference!" Visser One raged. "And if you weren't incompetent and a traitor to the empire you'd have cleaned these vermin up before now!"

The massive snake head grinned an evil grin as it towered above us. <No doubt the Council of Thirteen will certainly enjoy hearing your excuses for failure.>

"What the Council will hear is how you've allowed a handful of morphing Andalites to go unpunished!"

<You'll lose Leeran for us yet, you half-human fool!>

"Like you've already lost Earth, despite the fact I handed it over to you in perfect shape?"

It was bizarre. You have to understand that

there was a huge, roaring battle going on between my friends and the Hork-Bajir. And I was standing there, having just punched out a Leeran. But all the two vissers seemed to care about was trashing each other.

Politics. I guess it's the same everywhere.

And then a third thing happened. A massively loud alarm that went off. An automated voice bellowed from speakers up in the rafters.

"Brr-REEET! Brr-REEET! Warning. Warning. Containment seals will shut down in three minutes. Extreme hazard. Countdown beginning. Countdown will be in intervals of ten seconds. Thank you and have a nice day!"

I don't know which stunned me more. The fact that there was an announcement heralding the fact that a billion gallons of water were going to come rushing in. Or the fact that the computerized voice had wished us a nice day.

I wanted to laugh. Or at least say something. But I just ran.

CHAPTER 25

"Containment failure in two minutes and fifty seconds. Have a nice day!"

<Hah hah hah hah,> Visser Three laughed. <Water rushing in, and you're stuck in that weak human body, Visser One. Is that my promotion I see coming?>

Visser One was red with rage. But she turned and ran toward the office building.

<Yes, you'd better hurry and turn off your computer!> Visser Three crowed. <If you are able! These Andalites are devils with computers, you know. Hah hah hah!>

"Containment failure in two minutes and forty seconds. Have a nice day!"

I was off and running. A bloodied Jake saw

me coming. Rachel was just tossing a crumpled Hork-Bajir aside.

<Nice of you to drop by, Marco,> she said. <Did you at least get rid of Visser One for us?>

<No,> I said curtly.

<You okay?> Jake asked me privately.

<No. I'm not. But what we have to focus on is getting out of here.>

Just then, down from the sky, something huge plummeted toward us. Something huge and poison yellow, aiming right for Ax.

<Ax, look out!>

Visser Three's massive jaws opened wide, ready to snap the Andalite up. But Ax dodged nimbly aside.

<I am not human, Marco. It's not so easy to sneak up on me,> Ax said calmly.

"Containment failure in two minutes and ten seconds. Have a nice day."

Visser Three reared back up and aimed once more for Ax. This time the massive head came down faster. Ax jumped left and tried to whip his tail at the creature's head. But he tripped. One hoof caught on a piece of debris. He lurched. He stumbled.

<Got you!> Visser Three cried in glee.

The jaws closed around Ax!

But then, with Ax literally in his mouth, Visser Three stopped suddenly.

He stopped because a very large, very angry grizzly had just grabbed his midsection.

<Let him go,> Rachel growled. <Let him go or I'll rip you in two.>

I was shocked that she was speaking to Visser Three. But I guess she had no choice.

The visser kept his jaws still. He could have chomped Ax in half. But he didn't.

<It's a standoff, Andalite,> Visser Three said. <You have me, and I have your fellow terrorist here. But the water will be pouring in soon, and you'll drown in that body.>

<Let him go!> Rachel said and tightened her grip till her claws drew yellow-and-green ooze from the punctures in the snake body.

<I guess we have a negotiation here,> the visser said.

I stepped in close, took careful aim at the snake head, drew back my arm, powered the massive bunched muscles in my neck and shoulders, put four hundred pounds of weight into it and punched the visser in the nose.

<Negotiate this,> I said, as my fist met the squishy-soft snake snout. The visser's snake eyes flew open. His jaw flew open. He sort of hovered for a few seconds. Then his head hit the ground.

He slithered, mostly unconscious, back into the water. A trail of green ooze marked where he'd been.

Ax himself was covered with the same disgusting green slime.

<Thank you,> he said, calmly.

"Containment failure in one minute and forty seconds. Have a nice day."

<We have to get out of here!> I yelled.

Tobias flapped up off the head of a screaming Hork-Bajir. <Time to bail, boys and girls!>

"Containment failure suspended at one minute and forty seconds. Have a nice day."

<What?>

<It's Visser One!> Cassie said, loping over to us, a wolf who'd been through a bad half hour. She was cut in more places than I could count.

<You should have finished her off when you had the chance, Marco!> Rachel raged. <Now I'll take care of it.>

She lowered her humongous, furry bulk to the ground and went barreling away on all fours back toward the building. Ax ran with her, his deadly tail held high.

<Marco, you know what they're going to do,> Jake said urgently.

I nodded my thick gorilla head. <Yeah, Jake. I know.>

<It's your call,> Jake said neutrally.

<Yeah.>

I just stood there, frozen, as Rachel and Ax reached the door of the building.

<Jake. You and Cassie and Tobias morph, okay? I have to go and . . . I don't know.>

<Go,> Jake said. <We'll have gills within a minute. Marco?>

<Yeah?>

<Do what's right. Forget about what anybody thinks. Do what's right.>

That's my friend Jake. That's his answer to anything, I guess: Do what's right. And somehow, he always seems to know just what that is. Or at least he thinks he does. Jake's a natural hero. Heroes always know what's right.

Me? I'm a comedian. All I know is what's funny. And what isn't.

CHAPTER 26

I found them in her office. That's where she had gone to override the computer. She stood, defiant behind her desk, with a handheld Dracon beam.

TSEEEWWW!

She fired! The blazing hot beam of light burned a neat semicircle out of Rachel's right shoulder.

"Rrrroooowwwwrrrr!" she bellowed in pain.

Visser One turned the Dracon beam on Ax.

FWAPPP!

Ax's tail blade was too fast for me to see. But I saw the gash on Visser One's human arm. And I saw the Dracon beam drop.

Rachel was on her in a flash. Grizzlies can be

very fast when they need to be, or when they are mad. And Rachel was mad.

Her sheer momentum knocked Visser One sprawling across the room. And when she tried to stand up, Rachel was over her.

It was no contest. Bear against human. Morphed bear against human-Controller. It was hopeless. Visser One might as well have been a rag doll. With one sweeping blow of her daggered paw, Rachel could knock Visser One's head from her shoulders.

<NO!> I yelled.

Rachel swiveled her head and stared at me with nearsighted bear eyes. <Shut up, Marco!>

<I said no! Don't do it!>

<She's a Yeerk visser,> Ax pointed out calmly.

<No,> I said again. <She's my mother.>

It seemed like a very long time during which no one moved. Visser One, my mother, had heard nothing, of course. I'd thought-spoken only to Rachel and Ax.

<Your mother's dead,> Rachel said.

<No. I thought she was. This is her. Or *was* her. And maybe will be again someday if . . . if she lives.>

Rachel hesitated. Then, almost angrily, but really with very little force for a bear, she tossed my mother's body aside.

<Thanks,> I said.

But Ax was not so easily convinced. <Marco, she remains a danger to us.>

<Maybe not,> I said. <Look.> I pointed to the big round window that looked out onto the sea. There, just beyond the glass bubble, was a monstrous yellow serpent. Visser Three.

<He saw us spare her life,> I said. <How do you think Visser Three would interpret that?>

<He'll think she's a traitor,> Ax said instantly. <It's what he wants to believe. And when he sees that we've let her live, it will be all the evidence he needs.>

<I'm sorry, Marco,> Rachel said. The violent frenzy of battle was drained from her now. <I didn't know.>

<Shut up, Xena,> I said harshly.

<Hey, I'm trying to be nice.>

<I know. So shut up.>

Ax had gone back to the computer. <She's locked me out. It could take me ten minutes to bypass.>

The movement was just a blur out of the corner of my eye. I had no time to yell. I just saw Visser One — my mother — grab the Dracon beam she had dropped. She rolled with it, brought it up, and aimed it squarely at Rachel.

Too far away to grab her!

Instinct took over. Not gorilla instinct, but human instinct. The lightning-quick, intelligent, and ruthless decision-making that had allowed Homo sapiens to rule over all the other animals.

I snatched up a chair. It was heavy. Steel and leather.

And I flung it with all the power in my gorilla arms. I meant to throw it at my mother. I missed. Or maybe I meant to miss. Maybe I'll never know for sure.

But the chair flew fast and hard.

It hit the bubble window.

CRUNCH!

The glass wasn't shattered, only cracked. But the pressure of the water beyond was too great. It began to seep and then to spray through.

My mother flinched.

TSEEEEWWW! The Dracon beam missed.

Rachel reacted swiftly, slapping Visser One with the back of her paw. A nasty blow, but not a fatal one.

<That window is going to break!> Ax yelled.

<We have to get out of here!> Rachel yelled. <Now, now, now!>

<I have to save her!> I cried.

<Run, you idiot, or no one will be saved!> Rachel cried.

CRRR-UMPH! The window exploded inward! FWOOOOOOSH!

It was like standing with your face two inches from a fire hose. The power of the water was insane! It was like getting hit by a log.

I was instantly knocked off my feet, swirling and swirling in the insane, foaming avalanche of water.

The room was a tornado. Water whipped everything around in a spiral. And then something long and brilliant yellow came shooting into the room.

Visser Three! The sudden suction had overwhelmed him and drawn him in, like lint being sucked by a vacuum cleaner.

The office door popped out like a cork. Rachel, Ax, me, and Visser Three's huge sea serpent morph went flying down the hall. It was like we'd been shot out of a cannon.

Down the hallway as the walls collapsed outward.

FWOOOSH!

Out through the annihilated wall of the building. The water spread out a little then and I could see where I was. I looked for her and saw her floating facedown a hundred yards away.

I tried to swim to her. But the current was too powerful.

<Morph!> Rachel yelled.

But I had already begun. I was halfway to human again. I saw Rachel, mostly still a bear, go spinning by.

I caught a glimpse of something with pebbly green-and-yellow skin moving easily through the raging tidal wave. Its tentacles seemed perfectly designed for resisting the current.

The Leeran!

He was heading for my mother.

To save her? To destroy her? To capture her so that Visser Three could enjoy watching her suffer?

I don't know. Because I was swept into the dock and sank down into the deep water.

I gasped desperately for air, my human lungs on fire!

And I searched for the shark inside me.

CHAPTER 27

The sharks were waiting for us. The super-hammerheads. They were there, circling the facility. I don't know how, but somehow they'd been put on alert. Or maybe the destruction of the facility just had them agitated.

<Here they come!> Cassie warned.

If you have ever wondered what fear looks like, I can draw you a picture: It's a dozen hammerhead sharks looking at you and grinning their evil, downturned hammerhead grins.

On they came. And I didn't care. I didn't care. I wanted battle. I wanted pain. And I wanted to inflict pain. I wasn't the calm, emotionless shark. I was a boy who'd watched his mother die. Again.

I didn't wait for the sharks to reach me. I

kicked my elegant hammerhead tail and I went for the nearest, biggest shark I could see.

We closed, like two colliding cars. Face-to-face. Hammer-to-hammer.

I twisted my hammer head and planed sideways, then twisted instantly back. My foe had tried to react. But he was only a smart shark, while I was a human. I knew how he would react, and I was ready.

Too late, he saw my mouth open. Too late, he saw the rows of serrated triangles. I bit. I closed my jaws down with enough power to sever a leg.

I ripped a chunk out of that shark and yelled, <Yes! Yes! Come and get some more!>

<Marco! Stop it!> Jake shouted.

I twisted till I was upside down, kicked, turned my head, and grabbed the tail of my opponent. I sawed my teeth and removed the upper lobe of the shark's tail.

<Marco! I said stop it!>

Suddenly a shark body slammed into me. It knocked me sideways. My opponent swam away, definitely not interested in fighting anymore.

I turned toward this new shark.

<It's me, Marco,> Jake said. <It's me. They're leaving. They've broken off. They've lost the signal from the facility and they are escaping.>

I just stared at him. At the shark he was.

<It's over, Marco. Let's get out of here.>

The blood lust faded. I looked around and saw the last of the engineered sharks heading away.

Huge bubbles were erupting from the underwater facility. Explosions rocked the sea, like echoing hammer blows through the water. The hologram that disguised the facility shimmered and disappeared as we swam away from the absolute horror.

We saw Visser Three, a distant yellow ribbon, snaking away.

I felt a tingling, watery feeling in my head. The control chip was being liquidated. Ax had said it would happen when the facility's computer decided the end had come.

The Yeerks are good at destroying evidence. The chips in all the sharks were liquidating. No fisherman would ever catch a shark with alien technology in its head.

<They're done for,> Cassie said.

<Hopefully, at least Visser One didn't escape,> Tobias said. <I'd like to think she is down there, trying to figure out how to hold her breath right about now.>

It was just the kind of thing I would have said.

Jake and Ax were silent. I knew Jake would tell Cassie now. If he didn't, Rachel would. They would all know. Jake and Rachel and Ax already knew.

They knew that my heart was ripping apart. They knew that I was crying. Or crying as well as any shark could.

I had lost my mother once. Now I'd lost her again. Unless . . .

I pictured the Leeran swimming toward her. Had she made it? No. It wasn't possible.

We swam away. We swam toward shore, where we would be human once again and go back to our lives. Back to home and homework. Back to saying good night to a picture of my mother.

But nothing would ever be the same now. How could it be? They would all know.

I felt the energy drain out of me. I was exhausted. Exhausted and defeated. I waited for someone to say something nice. Something sweet and comforting. Something that they would never have said to the old Marco.

<Hey. I just heard something,> Rachel said. <Mechanical. Like . . . hey! It's the same sound the sub made. That transparent sub. I heard its engines.>

<I don't hear anything,> Tobias argued.

<It's coming from over in this direction,> Rachel said. <Over closer to me.>

I didn't hear anything, either. Maybe Rachel was just making it up. Maybe she was trying to give me some tiny hope to cling to. It didn't sound like something Rachel would do. But there are hidden depths to Rachel. There are times she'll surprise you.

<Thanks, Xena,> I said.

You know, if she'd said, <You're welcome,> I'd have known it was a lie. That she hadn't heard a sub. That she was just trying to be nice.

<Thanks for what? For hearing that sub? For paying more attention than you, Marco?> Rachel sneered in her usual Rachel sneer. <You know, possibly the reason I notice more than you do, Marco, is that I don't use half my brain making dumb jokes and the other half of my brain laughing at them.>

It was a pretty good shot. It made me laugh a little. I don't mind when the jokes are at my own expense. As long as they're funny.

Was it true? Had my mother made it to the sub and escaped? I don't know, and I guess I wasn't totally sure what I wanted the truth to be.

If she was gone . . . really, really gone, then I could be a normal person again. I could be sad and then put it behind me. I could be free.

If she was still alive, still trapped, then I was still trapped, too. I still had to try and save her. I would still be a prisoner of hope.

<I'll ask you this just once more, and then never again, because I know how you are about people feeling sorry for you,> Jake said privately

so no one else could hear. <Are you okay, Marco?>

Like I always say, you have to decide whether you think life is tragedy or comedy. I long ago decided to look for the joke in life.

And now I had to decide whether, in my own mind, she was dead or still alive. Suddenly I had this flash. This picture in my head. Me and her. Me and my mom. My real mom, free, no longer a Controller. It would be far in the future. Years from now, maybe. Me and her and my dad would sit down together and talk about how it had been. About all the stuff that had happened. All the secrets and despair. All the fear. All the anger and hopelessness. We'd remember it all.

And then, slowly but surely, we'd talk less about how horrible it had all been. We'd start talking about the strange stuff. The weird stuff. The stuff that we could laugh at, now that it was all over.

See, it was my mom who taught me that the world was funny.

And if she was alive, we'd maybe still get that day in the future to sit down and laugh together.

<I'm fine, Jake,> I said. <And I'll be better. When she's free again.>

Don't miss

ᎪᏁᎥᎷᎾᎡᏢᎻᏕ ®

#16 The Warning

I'm sure it was a beautiful house. But I didn't really see it. All I saw with my dim rhino-vision were walls and doorways. But at least we'd been right to guess that there were wide hall-ways. Wide enough for me to barrel down like a . . . well, like a rhinoceros.

And the ceilings were high enough that To-bias, Cassie, and Marco could fly down them, searching madly from room to room. Searching with vision greater than human vision and hear-ing that could pick up the sound of a gopher belching from a distance the length of a football field.

They used me to open doors.

<Jake, open this door,> Marco would say. I'd turn where he showed me, shove my massive bony face forward, and the door would explode in splinters.

CRRR-UNCH-BANG!

<We are trashing this man's home,> Cassie

said. <I sure hope he is a Controller after all this.>

<He can afford to have his doors fixed,> Marco said.

<That's not the point,> Cassie said. Then, <Jake, open this door, please.>

CRRRR-UNCH-BANG!

<Nothing,> Tobias complained. <Nothing, nothing, nothing! Nothing in any of these rooms, and there may be a hundred rooms in this place.>

<Tobias is right. We are out of time,> Cassie said.

<This isn't the way to do it,> I said. <We can't just search room to room. It could take hours. We need to figure this out. How do we find Ax and Rachel? Where would they be?>

<In the last place we look,> Marco grumbled. <Or at least . . . wait a minute! Wherever they are, they'll be guarded.>

<Yes!> I said. <Of course. We just rampage till we see something well guarded.>

<I'll head upstairs,> Tobias said.

He zoomed away and up a large staircase. I lumbered along into a vast open living room area. I stomped on through. I tried not to crush too much furniture, but I was big and half-blind, so I kept hearing the crunch of wood and the shatter of glass and pottery in my wake.

<Up here!> Tobias yelled.

Then, not as loud as before, but still loud enough . . . BLAM! BLAM!

<Tobias!>

<I'm okay! But I found an area with two big guys with big guns. It's upstairs.>

I tried to turn around and head back to the stairs, but then Marco yelled.

<Uh-oh! Guys coming up behind us. Man, how many gunmen does this lunatic hire? Jake, we have to go *through* these guys to get back to the stairs!>

<I got guys on my tail!> Tobias yelled down from upstairs.

I spun around and wiped out a couch in the process. <This way?!>

<No, a little left!>

I turned and annihilated a coffee table. Then I charged. I couldn't tell the difference between the men and various pole lamps and bookcases, except when they moved. The blur drew my eye, and I smelled humans.

I lowered my head and charged.

BLAM! BLAM!

Shotgun pellets stung but didn't penetrate beneath my outer skin.

POP! POP! POP! POP!

I was hit. I staggered. I felt the bullet from the handgun tear into my right shoulder. A second slug lodged in the bone of my face.

I hit the guy with the gun. I was mad. I lowered my horn and I tossed my head back. He went flying back over my shoulder.

"Ya-ah-AHHHHHH!"

The other man jumped aside. I think he was fumbling to reload his shotgun. I sideswiped him and knocked him into the wall. Then I was out of the room, back into the hallway, tearing along back to the staircase.

I was bleeding. And I was weakening on my right side. My right front leg was moving slower. The bullet in my face must have ricocheted off. I felt pain there, but not the heaviness I felt in my shoulder.

I came to the stairs and tried to charge straight up. But rhinos were never meant for climbing stairs. My legs wouldn't lift high enough. My weight and momentum were too much. The wooden stairs splintered.

BLAM! BLAM!

<Tobias! What's going on up there?>

<I'm leading these guys around in circles and they're blowing the crap out of the walls and ceiling trying to shoot me.>

<I can't make the stairs. We need more firepower. Marco, Cassie, morph! Tobias, keep it up. Keep leading 'em on.>

A bird trapped in a house, being chased by

two guys with shotguns. Had I just sentenced Tobias to death?

I started to demorph as fast as I could. But
while my thought-speak was still functioning,
something occurred to me. <Rachel! Ax! Can you
guys hear me? Rachel! Ax!>

< . . . unh . . . what?>

<Who is that?>

< . . . unh . . . it is me, Aximili,> Ax said.

He sounded dazed. I wasn't surprised. <Ax!
Demorph! Time's up!>

<But there are humans here watching me,
Prince Jake.>

Another decision. <Just do it, Ax, we're coming for you! Do you — > My thought-speak went
dead as I became more human than rhinoceros.

<Yes, Prince J — > Ax fell silent.

I was shrinking. My armored flesh became
tender human skin. My face was flat and deli-
cate. But my legs could handle stairs. I still
heard the sounds of gunfire from upstairs. And
the sad thing was, I was glad. As long as they
were still shooting, it meant Tobias wasn't dead
yet.

Marco and Cassie were just becoming human
again. They were three foot tall lumps of feathers
and shrinking beaks and emerging skin.

One wrong move and Tobias was gone. Ax

might be demorphing in front of people who might be Controllers. Rachel . . . no one knew whether Rachel was even conscious and capable of demorphing. Or alive at all. And now the three of us were utterly vulnerable, weak, pathetic.

I just kept thinking: This wasn't even supposed to be a very dangerous mission. And now, we were as close to being wiped out as we'd ever been.

"Cshom on!" I said, slurring my words with a mouth that was not human yet. "No chime kleft!"

I started up the stairs, staggering on my shifting, changing legs. The joints weren't right. The toes weren't toes, and my ankles seemed to have no flexibility. But time was up. I dragged myself up those stairs, hoping desperately that I had not killed us all. . . .